Widow

ALSO BY MICHELLE LATIOLAIS

Even Now
A Proper Knowledge

Widow

STORIES

MICHELLE LATIOLAIS

BELLEVUE LITERARY PRESS

NEW YORK

BELLEVUE LITERARY PRESS
NEW YORK

BELLEVUE LITERARY PRESS

NEW YORK

First published in the United States in 2011 by
Bellevue Literary Press
New York

FOR INFORMATION ADDRESS:
Bellevue Literary Press
NYU School of Medicine
550 First Avenue
OBV 640
New York, NY 10016

This book was published with the generous support of
Bellevue Literary Press's founding donor the Arnold Simon Family Trust
and the Bernard & Irene Schwartz Foundation.

Cataloging-in-Publication Data is available from the Library of Congress

Book design and type formatting by Bernard Schleifer
Manufactured in the United States of America
ISBN 978-1-934137-30-7
FIRST EDITION
1 3 5 7 9 8 6 4 2

For Joy Harris

Contents

❖

Queen of Swords (Regina di spade)
"connotes widowhood, separation and mourning",
15th centuryHand-painted on heavy cardboad
From the Visconti-Sforza tarot,
The Pierpont Morgan Library, New York

Widow

❖

She is sitting on the examining table wrapped in a paper gown, one of those dull pretty colors chosen for women, mauve, and she might as well be trying to cover herself with a refrigerator box, as the paper gown is all eaves and walls and encloses her like a shed or fallen timbers. She peers from this structure, the gown's neck up around her jaw, which she holds down so she can answer his questions without talking through a paper mask.

"Yes," she says, "No," and they are the same answer —yes, she has not had sexual intercourse for almost two years; no, she has not had sexual intercourse for almost two years—and he shakes his head, the gynecologist, and says it yet again, looks up at her. "Wow," he says. "Wow." He scoots around a bit on his castered stool, continues to read the chart; she is a new patient, and the nurse practitioner has made copious notes. "What did you do," he says, "kill your husband?" It is a quip—she hears this—a quip, an icebreaker, out of his mouth so quickly it's obvious he hasn't thought for an instant what he is saying. Perhaps he's used to treating divorced women who are angry, or unmarried women in Los Angeles, of which there seem to be many—dating, not dating—perhaps he's used to commiserating about "what jerks men are." She doesn't know, but she can't find it in herself to punish him for this comment either, can't bring herself to grind in just how callous a remark it is, how unbelievably out of line. Maybe what saves him is that she had a happy marriage. She knows that everyone says stupid things, knows how to forgive and be forgiven, a happy marriage.

She looks down at him on his stool. She keeps a mild look on her face, a look she learned from a colleague of hers, a look with hang time in it, a look that allows just enough time for you to gather to your narrow wits that you've said something *terribly* stupid, time-stoppingly stupid. Certainly he hears what has just flown from his mouth, and he starts to say something—perhaps to apologize—changes his mind, looks down, flips to the second page of the chart, looks up, scoots back against the wall, hikes his loafered foot up onto the stool rung, asks, "So, what do you think is going on?" and she thinks this a smart opening for a male gynecologist to offer a female patient, the authority of her own body, but then, before she can answer, he says again, "Wow, two years, you haven't had sex in two years?" and he fixes her with a look, and she realizes that it is her turn to say "Wow."

He thinks she is lying.

Wandering is better than place sometimes, than home, than destination. Sometimes she can eke out the idea that wandering is possibility, chance, serendipity—he might be there, that place she didn't think to look, hadn't worked hard enough to find; and sometimes wandering is better because she forces herself to move, and one day, at a neighborhood mall, she wanders into Barnes & Noble, a bookstore she rarely patronizes, and she stands before the shelf of etiquette books and pulls down each book and turns to "Widow," to "Death," to all the fine advice and less fine insistences, her favorite being "A widow never wears pearls . . . or if she dares to, they must be black or gray."

Sometimes wandering is not better; it's the horror of having no place she is going, no place he needs her to be, wants her to be, no one wanting her the way he wanted her. Then she sleeps, long blacked-out hours, her head beneath pillows, the quilt, and when she wakes, her pink pearls, sinuous on the vanity, comfort her; there are advantages to living in such an oblivious culture.

She has known what the word *widow* meant since she was seventeen years old, sitting uncomfortably in a course titled Women and Appearance, team-taught by two butch lesbians disdainful of anything she recognized as female. One of the professors occupied a wheelchair awkwardly, almost sideways, and had since birth, cerebral palsy or MS—she would never know—and the professor's misogyny was spectacular and blistering and successfully kept her from claiming any allegiance to feminism until years later, when she sorted herself out from the professor's furious projections, equations that had gone something along these lines of:

—her high-heeled shoes were a mindless acceptance of hobbling, on par with MS or palsy

—her lipstick, a shroud cast upon vital, unmaimed, unflawed flesh

—her slimness—genetic as it was—somehow more willfully derived through deprivation to please a male world

Her handicapped professor knew more deeply than any of them the chains of being female. What was tricky—and she knew this even then—was that she believed the professor *had* suffered more than she would ever suffer, no matter what happened to her, no matter what had happened to her now; and she knew from this class so long ago that *widow* meant "empty" in Sanskrit, and *this* empty could only be meant sexually, no hot dog for your bun, no sausage for your muff, that sort of thing, but she didn't yet have that humor at seventeen, was not yet equipped with the flippant bawdiness she came to admire as truly feminist and unapologetic and unabashedly sexual.

"So, what do you think is going on?" he asks her again.

She bolts her food now. Not to bolt her food is to take enough time to lose her appetite. Her periods have stopped, she has lost so much weight. She stands most evenings in her kitchen, shoveling in food, feeding herself as rapidly as she can swallow. Her mother said to them so often as children, "Don't stand there feeding like animals at the trough. For God's sake, sit down and eat like civilized human beings," and she has tried, has set the small table in the breakfast room with candles and a napkin, silverware, a wineglass, a water glass, moved a bowl of fruit or flowers, some centerpiece, fanned out magazines, all manner of enticement to normalcy, but this decorum is in such stark contrast to the ruin within her. She sits down to it, but she might as well be a stone god made offerings to, the food still there in the morning in the folds of her granite lap.

In filling out the medical history, there are the little boxes in which one places the check or the *X* or just blackens the space entirely, and when she gets to the choices "single" or "married," and there is no other box, she cannot mark either. Even dependable Leviticus weighs in on widows and aligns them with whores and divorced women and forbids priests from marrying such defiled creatures, chapter 21, verse 14, *And the Lord said unto Moses, a widow, or a divorced woman, or profane, or an harlot, these shall he not take: but he shall take a virgin of his own people to wife.* Since this is a gynecological medical history, she laughs aloud in the office, garners looks from the receptionist, wants very much the box that reads "whore, profane, harlot, widow," a catch-all box, and she intends every imaginable pun in the world by this.

More soberly, she writes in the word "widow."

It's not that she's being unreasonable about the questionnaire; rather, it's an attempt to give them some sense of her actual physical state. She has been surprised by grief, its constancy, its immediacy, its unrelenting physical pain.

Sometimes she is almost hysterical, as though every cell in her body were popping with excitement, ebullient, effervescent. At first this astonished her, this wave of wild nervous glee she swept forward on . . . but she came to understand the body could not withstand grief every waking moment, that the body would insist on a cessation for a time of the morbidity of grieving.

So, it could be that she was shrill and laughing, insistently laughing, a laughter that demanded itself into being, her mind leaping at any possible comment by someone, or any attribute that could be made a joke, funny, fodder for the laugh track, and she knew it to be happening when it happened, was conscious of the laughing faces around her, conscious as though she stood behind glass and the faces at once stared and laughed, their lips and eyes and mouths all laughing . . . and she could hear her body's desperate bull-horning. She supposed those around her recognized the merriment for the desperation it was . . . but did they know her body drove this ecstatic desperation forward?

And so, she will drive home after being at some gathering, a reception or a party, and she will feel her nerves sparking, nervously desultory, frayed with hysteria, and she will be ashamed of herself, will know that everyone has laughed out of politeness or the relief that she isn't an unhappy prospect to be around. What or whom can she trust now? She will say to herself, "You're trying too hard; you don't need to try so hard." But it isn't exactly that, either; it is her body insisting on whatever laughter provides.

"Exercise?" he asks, his back leaned up against the wall, his elbow resting on the chrome lid of one of the tall trash bins. HAZARDOUS, it reads. He has stopped looking at her chart and it now rests half on and half off the Formica counter. He sits forward abruptly, suggests for the second time "spinning," and she finally says, "I'm sorry, I don't know what you mean by 'spinning.' I walk a lot. In the mornings, early, several miles perhaps. I don't know."

"No gym?" he says, rising from his stool and pulling out the metal arms of the examining table, one on each side of her.

"No," and she thinks to say, *Not my thing, not my scene,* but she doesn't. She knows how odd she is to most people, and when there was someone at home to enfold her, a place where she belonged, it did not matter, but now she stops from adding fuel to anyone's sense of her, says as little as possible.

"It's a twisting machine," he tells her, "for toning the midsection, but you sit on it—I don't know why it's called 'spinning.'"

"No," she says quickly, precipitously, "no spinning, no bike riding, I really just walk. . . ." And she is about to say *and I do a lot of my own housework,* but she doesn't say this, either, knows in Los Angeles that might be even weirder than saying you don't frequent a gym, an admission, really, of being down on your luck, in straitened circumstances—something you'd never admit in fantasy town—but housework, it's exercise, and that is all she means to establish.

BIG UNIQUE SOFA!! Three words across the top of a flyer tacked up to a telephone pole on the corner near her house. This has made her laugh out loud. BIG UNIQUE SOFA and a few exclamation marks and a telephone number and maybe there was a price—she does not remember— really she remembers just the words BIG UNIQUE SOFA and the exclamation marks. Was there a band of little slips with the telephone number fluttering in the wind made by the traffic? She cannot remember that, either.

What could such an item promise? she asks herself. What could possibly be unique about a sofa? All the sofas I've known, she muses, all the gin joints . . . and you choose this. But then she is thinking about the sofa, the couch, in the therapist's office in Brentwood, the chenille throw spread across its seat, to cover stains or to prevent stains, she cannot tell which, but the six or seven times she leaves the office, she straightens it, pulls it taut again, doesn't like the throw there, doesn't like that it retains an impression of her. The therapist tells her every time not to worry about it, that she'll fix it, but she does not want a doctor straightening out a chenille throw after she leaves . . . something unnervingly domestic, assertively domestic. It bothers her enough that she has left the therapist with notes about her life, like hair or nail clippings left behind in a salon. It's not rational; she doesn't insist that it is, or even that it should be. She doesn't trust this blur of the professional and personal, cannot appreciate this exchange of money for her unguarded thoughts and feelings, doesn't trust professional ethics over codes of friendship or family—and she feels she has done her duty to her family by "seeing a therapist," and when the suggestion comes from the doctor, as she knew it ultimately would, that she take antidepressants, she leaves the office and never returns. She is deeply confused by someone studying someone else's mind and wanting to alter it chemically at the same time. BIG UNIQUE SOFA.

So impossible to go to doctors. He quarrels with every surmise the physician's assistant has made, says no, no, he doesn't think it's peri-menopausal. "No, no," he snaps, "throw that cream away; it's useless," and she is happy to, has read its prescription insert, the cancer warnings, but she has also spent money on it, at his office's advice, and she has suffered for several weeks beyond an initial visit with the physician's assistant. There is no apology for this mis-diagnosis, and certainly he doesn't cover for his own assistant, and she finds this astounding, the flipness, and she is very, very annoyed and trying to keep a lid on it, trying not to take his head off.

Leaving her attorney's office one day, they are both standing, about to approach the door, and he reaches for her hand, which rises from her side in the habit of shaking hands—is in his hand instantly, a matter of physical convention—and then she flinches, her entire body electrical, spastic, and she pulls her hand back, shrinking from his touch.

She understands only after she is safely out of the huge lush offices and down the tremendous shaft of the elevator, into the shadowy parking garage and alone in the clean dark plushness of her husband's car that she has not been touched by anyone in a month, even to shake hands, even an arm across her shoulder . . . not touched, and her body is so un-used to not being touched, is still so searching and desperate, frantic for his presence, his hold, and now she has flinched at the touch of a man whom she likes very much, and who has helped her—has helped her to stay alive, as she would not be had he not agreed to represent her.

He is no idiot. For one thing, he is a plaintiff's attorney, and either they have empathy by nature or they learn it, and she knows he has not missed a flinch, a tremor, her whisking her hand out of his. He has not missed a thing. Also—because he has rescued her, because he has lent credence to what she knows has caused her husband's death—she is a little in love with him, as anyone is with one's rescuer, anyone desperate for relief, and lonely.

She is with Portia at a party, a dinner, and they are laughing, lost for a moment from dead husbands, from workmen who now stand too long in the kitchen, looking around, free from lawyers who won't return phone calls, or from personal bankers now slow to respond . . . and so Portia and she will be out, and they will finally be laughing, sprung, and someone without fail will say, "Ah, the merry widows!"

They will stop laughing.

They will look at him.

They will look back at each other.

They will wait quietly until that person leaves.

They will say nothing.

Sorrow in her is so pervasive, so stultifying, she is slow to turn to anger. A lot of people's lives are spared because of this.

She is instructed one day by huge block letters across a new billboard to OUTLIVE YOUR SPOUSE, and then in smaller letters beneath, reads the phrase "The Antioxidant Power of Pomegranate Juice." She is not offended by the ad, nor exercised, nor upset; she is just perplexed by its utter stupidity, its puerile mindlessness. It's an ad for POM, and the *O* of POM is made with a heart instead of a circle. The heart is completely mechanistic, completely, in this ad, a designation for a muscle and its pumping abilities, its bloody chambers. She understands the hip young advertising team sitting around a big table thinking OUTLIVE

YOUR SPOUSE hysterically funny, sit-com funny, the appeal of one-upmanship for all those years of marital misery—she understands there are marriages like that, but what she can't understand is how the copy wasn't tabled, a funny idea that is ultimately vicious.

Marianne Wiggins says it best in a novel of hers: To love someone is to agree to die twice in a lifetime, to outlive nothing. What happens when one outlives a spouse is a shelf-life, gourd-like existence, dumb fleshy pumps . . . dumber ads.

One morning she wakes at 4:00 A.M. and stares into the empty darkness for a long time until she finally gets up and goes to the bathroom. The May 2004 *Playboy* is there in the basket in front of the toilet; a preternaturally blonde Pam Anderson is on the cover. She takes the magazine back to bed with her and reads the interview with Johnny Depp, and it is not as interesting as it should be, or perhaps she is less interested because she knows already that Keith Richards of the Rolling Stones served as a model for Depp's portrayal of Captain Jack Sparrow in *Pirates of the Caribbean*. She wants the interview to touch on the problems with the Disney producers when Depp arrived on the set with several of his teeth capped in gold. There is no mention of any of this, of the filming being stopped, or of the premiere being buried in Anaheim, California, because Disney thought the film a colossal flop, and Depp's performance fey, unpalatable, homosexual. The interview is a "pine float," as one of her stepfathers used to say, a glass of water with a toothpick in it. Nobody's telling the real story, and Depp's agent is probably there in the interview-editing room, making sure the next movie with Disney is not compromised. It is all so boring, so banal; she feels embarrassed for Depp.

She searches for the fiction but, before finding it, lights upon the requisite Buck Brown cartoon. She and her husband had many a conversation about Buck Brown's cartoons, as they almost always depict a sexually ravenous crone of a woman, a grandmother going for someone's gonads like nobody's business, a real predator. May's cartoon depicts a young man in an airport concourse with granny on her knees rapturously reaching into his pants for his privates. A blue-suited security guard restraining a German shepherd whispers conspiratorially into the young man's ear, "I thought you'd like to know, sir, she's not part of airport security." Both of the male faces—those of the security guard and the man being sexually accosted—have a surprised witlessness about them.

There is a middle-aged woman's face just beyond the shoulder of the young man—just a face in the crowd—but she wears the same down-turned line of a mouth as he does. She has little black dots for eyes and stares well over the head of granny into the distance, stoic and sexless.

Buck Brown's granny is not what she wants to see this morning at 4:20 A.M.: yet another depiction of a woman without sexual liaison or, more profoundly, a woman without sexual permission, the butt of the joke, and worse, her appetites disgusting, outlandish, and yet condescended to, tolerated, an embarrassment everyone must just endure.

She knows she is beginning to marmorealize into that character called "widow," untouchable, dark, by definition unhappy, sexless. Her body is fighting for her, for some existence it recognizes as oxygen, water, sustenance.

So impossible to go to doctors.

The Long Table

❖

At the wedding he had said to the young woman, "The children are so beautiful."

Later that evening, the young woman standing in the doorway, looking—everyone gone from the long table, the bride and groom, the parents, the brothers and sisters and their children, all gone, and the table with its silent marimba of glasses filled or emptied to various levels, wine and water and pomegranate punch, all quiet, though several times throughout the evening knife blades had been tapped sharply against the crystal bowls, each resonator different according to the level and to the drink, another toast, "Allow me," and even the beautiful children, so watchful of decorum, had tapped their short glasses filled with punch, had said, "I want to make a toast, too," or "Now it's my turn to say something," and they had stood and said astonishing things: "Will Uncle Carlos still double-kiss me now that he's married?" and "I think you should have a baby next week, okay? I think tomorrow would be too soon."

Uproarious laughter had ensued. The table so quiet now, so still the crumbs on the table, the half-eaten rolls, the twenty white napkins tossed into tiny heaps, the table so deeply quiet, a teaspoon here, one there canted up onto a saucer, a red carnation very rakishly leaning up out of a wineglass, and there, there beneath the lower leaves of the centerpiece, a dough lioness and lion crafted by an aunt from moistened bread crumb, the lion's mane cleverly a disk of golden crust etched with a fork tine. "Look, look!" the children had screamed. "Look at his mane. Make a giraffe," they begged, "a giraffe, a giraffe," and the aunt, her eyes trying to smile above cheeks lifeless with the exhaustion of her failing marriage, said no, she didn't really have any sense of how to make a giraffe; he had taught her only the lion and the lioness. "Who, Tante, who?" "Long ago," she said, laughing, her ringed fingers beginning to mold a wonderful giraffe's neck. "Oh, but you can, you can make a giraffe!" they shouted, and a little boy in a blue velvet weskit charged off to nab a bread roll as his mother's attention was turned, and prizing it in his small hands, he ran about the table to thrust it into his aunt's silken lap. "Long, long ago," she murmured, pulling bread from the roll, making the giraffe's neck longer and longer, and tapering the neck up into a head. "They have marvelous cheekbones, don't they? high and round, and funny horns with knobs on top. I don't think I can make horns," she said to them seriously. "Bread is not a very fine medium."

"Horns!" they shouted gleefully. "He must have horns! Horns! Horns! Horns!" they had shrilled, the table stood so vastly quiet now, the young woman could hear it all within the listening that was her gaze, and holding even longer this gaze, the young woman remembered an anguish in her aunt's laughter as she had devised giraffe horns from lily stamens. "Let's hope Marie doesn't mind us borrowing a few from her centerpiece," the aunt said, carefully boring two holes in the giraffe's white head with a fork tine and pushing the stamens in, the horns hilariously long and lopping about like bells on a jester's hat.

When she began to cry, they made a bower around her of small arms. "Tante, make a zebra," they said. "Make a tiger—a monkey—a bear—" It was as though they knew to keep her making things within the world, to keep her there; she could not have stood it had they said they loved her. "Tante, make a snake! Yeah, a SNAKE!" they said, their eyes wide with anticipation, and it seemed all at once they all held rolls in their hands. Her lap was mounded and overflowing with rolls. She laughed without exhaustion, without anguish, dipping her fingers into her wineglass and beginning to moisten the bread crumb. "A beautiful snake," she said with determination, "a beautiful snake with scales like rose petals." The children shook their heads very solemnly; they were in awe of their own powers of transformation.

Boys

✦

She is surprised by the amount of affection in the shabby upstairs room of a strip club in Las Vegas. An easy, gleeful warmth, the boys in their loose pull-away pants—or some already pulled away and so in nylon thongs—their penises half-erect and easy beneath the thin fabric, and the women uproarious, happy, probably mostly drunk but somehow unnegotiated nonetheless in their happiness at these beautiful boys in their laps, the gorgeous male loins held within their ringed fingers.

Boys, she thinks, *boys*, but they are men, young to be sure, more than likely gay, male hustlers at later hours perhaps, certainly that insistent retention of the adolescent boy in their grooming which translates to her, rightly or wrongly, as gay. And so not heterosexual, or not *just* heterosexual at any rate, and finally of far more interest is the tremendous amount of sweetness in the room, a suspension of stricture she hasn't ever seen before, and very different from the huge round tables downstairs with their center poles, the calculated variety of female types, the men pushed up to the tables with their wads of one-dollar bills, their drinks, their baseball hats reversed so they can bring their faces as close as possible to the naked crotches when they are offered, as close as is allowed without touching. And the men don't touch, don't even raise their arms unless it is to slide a bill across the table, and another: Over here! Please, over here! Wrap those legs around my shoulders! "I'm the one who needs pussy, over here!"

It's tired downstairs, an old contract, so old that it might be a covenant. It's all very carefully calculated, welcoming and friendly and the waggling, suggestive finger: Hey, big boy, snatch is over here. Just follow me, *And God looked on the earth, and behold, it was corrupt; for all flesh had corrupted their way upon the earth,* and plenty of Leviticus downstairs, too: *When any man has a discharge from his body, his discharge is unclean. . . . And every saddle on which the person with the discharge rides becomes unclean.* But upstairs is frontier unmapped by God.

Upstairs is shabby, though not tawdry, and there is very little money in view—in fact, none that she can see—and she hears no talk of money, though there must be plenty about, as several women have boys writhing in their laps, and certainly they are being paid for these hilarious displays of bodice-ripper romance, which no one that she can see is taking very sexually, and certainly not personally.

Upstairs there is a stage too, but it is long and L-shaped and without poles, more a runway for models, and used that way by the men, a lot of cock-of-the-walk strutting, amused, ironic, and then a retreat and a chair brought on up, and then, like dancing with a broom, there is the lap dance with a chair, and finally, finally, an ecstatic group of young women manage to rustle a bride-to-be up onto the stage, where she is sat giddily down and then much moved upon by the dancer, his vigorous legs astride her, the loose silken purse of his genitalia in her lap.

She knows a poem in which a poet writes about the desire to take his infant son's genitals in his mouth, not in any furtive act of fellatio, but rather as an expression—a measure—of overwhelming love and protectiveness.

She admires the bravery of penning the fullest measure of the heart, the bravery of throwing down into shards the tea set of moral convention and saying, "It is my heart that is exquisite, it is my heart!"

She understands the response of the mouth, the desire to take the child back into one's body, the terror that he is his own body now, sovereign—the terror that he is not yet his own body and may never actually be.

When she was eighteen years old, standing in a post office in San Francisco, she had turned to see a line out onto Fillmore Street, a line of boys, uncharacteristically boy-like, subdued, quiet-eyed, and she had finally asked the pudgy, pale-faced one behind her why they were all there and he had said, "Registering for Selective Service" in as manly a voice as he could muster. The war was Vietnam and the reports were getting uglier and America was coming around to the idea that it was losing—a truth that just didn't have a thing to wear from the wardrobe of national regalia.

She is not alone upstairs, would not have come here alone; doesn't look for trouble in those ways. He is with her, has ordered drinks, is smoking, his hand holding his cigarette the way his hand always holds his cigarette, snug against the knuckles of his middle fingers, the fingers fanned, his eyes narrowed, looking out over his fanned fingers. He is not uncomfortable, but he's not all that interested either, and this compels her. He has gay friends, so there is some other issue at work upstairs, perhaps only that he could be downstairs watching comely young women take their clothes off, something she doesn't blame him for liking—something she isn't particularly threatened by. Wouldn't he be dead if he didn't like that? She'd rather he not be dead.

Nonetheless, a snarly, odd tension insinuates itself between them. "Do you want to leave?" she asks, but not very seriously; they have just arrived. The table is loaded with drinks, a tip tray, her purse, his lighter, his cigarettes. It's like their nightstand in the hotel room; it looks like they've settled in. He is the only fully attired male in the room—or actually, there is a DJ who seems dressed, but he is up a plywood ramp, elevated with the sound system in a wire cage, and so not so much a part of the room as he is a surveillant orchestrator. "We can leave," she says. "It would be all right," she adds.

"When you're ready," he says, but how it has become all about her, her desires, she can't exactly figure. She wouldn't even know about this club if it weren't for him, and she assumes they are here because of curiosity on his part—their part—not something expressly for her. If it is expressly for her, this trek down the Strip past the famous casinos, well into the older, more somber blocks, she'd like to be in on the planning next time! Of course, she'd gone along, said, "Sure, let's see what it's all about." She's wearing black sling-back heels. She hadn't expected the club to be such a hike. It was windy outside, desert windy, that dry mausoleum chill the desert blows, and she is still a little unnerved, spooked, the chill weird for June. In her head were the cabbie's words from the airport, "Vegas is the safest town in America."

"Like Little Italy in New York," she joked.

"Yeah," he said, craning his head up to the rearview mirror, as though a woman who joked about power politics and human malice deserved a look. "Just like Little Italy."

The dancer is dark-haired, of medium build, and he runs his hand down her back, a tickle really, like a brother coming up behind and saying hello with his fingers. He leans over and whispers in her ear, "Whenever you're ready," and the waggish frisson of his hand on her back could make her ready, she muses . . . but ready for what?

She watches the dancer as he walks off, the saunter and occasional pivot in and around chairs, tables, his hand feathered across a bare, muscled back, perhaps his own lover toiling over a woman. There is something vaguely petulant in the hitch and glide of his walk, something seductive, but not conjured for her, though if she's caught up in his sweep, that's fine by him—it's a show, for God's sake, a show, and so she'll watch, sure she'll watch, amused, protective—she likes this easy affection within the multiplicity of sexualities.

"Whenever you're ready . . ."

"When you're ready . . ." and she realizes both her lover and the dancer have said almost precisely the same thing to her: Whenever you're ready to leave. Whenever you're ready to have a lap dance.

Strangely, the idea of motherhood occurs to her, ready for motherhood.

Tonight, before leaving their room for dinner and the clubs, he had switched on the television. A woman named Andrea Yates was in the news. She had given birth to five children in seven years, five children whom she had drowned earlier in the day, one after another in a bathtub in Texas, and later today, not much later, the news showed a sidewalk of Texan women screaming for Andrea Yates to be "fried." These women on the television screen were plump and blonde and fiercely righteous in their insistence. "Fry her!" they screamed in the bright Texas daylight. "Fry her!"

In this dim room upstairs in Las Vegas, there are women screaming all around her, boys riding their laps—these women are screaming with laughter, some beast unleashed in their hearts, too. *Whenever you're ready for a lap dance*, the boys are offering. *Whenever you're ready to leave*, her lover says, and above the huge electrical emission of the room she hears the voices of the Texan women. *Fry her*, they scream, *Fry her*.

She thinks about the colloquialism "to fry" for electrocution, the odd disparity between their righteousness and the slang they use to insist upon it. She assumes these women do not know that *fry* also means children, human offspring, *small fry*. "Children her," these women are screaming, "children her! Give her young ones. Give her spawn!"

She might be included in this fury, she, a woman sitting in a strip club in Las Vegas, watching beautiful young men hustle their bodies. *Fry her*, they might scream, because she feels no need to ask the question so earnestly voiced on the news: How could a mother murder her children? The more she learned about the case, standing in their hotel room, her eyes fixed on the television screen, the icier her clarity became.

There's footage of Russell Yates holding a press conference, his coolness, his righteousness, his religion. She thinks it took this extreme act on his wife's part to make him listen, and yet still he speaks, the mikes all held out to him, the notepads filling up with his words. But there were earlier notepads filled up with Andrea Yates's words, her confession, which she gave summarily, simply—which child she had drowned first, Paul, and then which next, Luke, and then John, and how old they were, and how she had laid them under a maroon blanket on the bed, though not the baby, whom she left floating face-down in the tub as she drowned the last and eldest son, Noah, blameless in his time, but drowned nonetheless. How grisly a detail, the one girl, Mary, a six-month-old infant, left to float beside her eldest brother, and why, after the other three had been laid out neatly on the bed?

When her lover leans across to ask her if she'd like a lap dance, no matter how ludicrous the notion is to her, it is, disturbingly, one of those moments in a relationship, one of those beginning-of-the-end moments, if either partner were to allow it to drive its tiny wedge. She can hear the words spoken tearfully to friends: "It seemed like a good idea at the time, or not a good idea, but something different, fun, a lark, for Christ's sake—it was a lark." She can imagine that the image of an essentially naked man moving over her body pushed deeper and deeper into the chair would be an image he couldn't shake, an image his heart would have no accommodation for, and she thinks this is true whether he loves her or not. She thinks he doesn't know this about himself. He asks about the lap dance as though he were asking about her desire for another drink, the lap dance and the offerings of the bar unnervingly equal in the register of his voice, and she can't think of anything she would find more absurd than this mock display of heated-up love-making happening athwart her legs. She laughs. "I don't think I'm up for that, but more to the point, are you?"

"Yeah," he says. *Yeah*, but it's hardly an affirmative, it's actually a *Maybe* or an *I don't know*. She wants to meddle with this confusion, wants to challenge him to understand the treachery of his offer and the menace of what would arise were she to take him up on it.

She looks across at him and he immediately looks down, laughs at himself. "Just being polite," he says.

"Maybe?" she says.

Walking toward her is a new dancer on the floor, tall, slender. "He's pretty beautiful," she says, and somehow her words are audible within the electronic din, dropping straight into the dancer's ears. His arms are astride the chair before she can hold her hands up to say, "No, you're like a page in a magazine. I was just admiring the pulchritude." His lips are whispering something near her cheek, a price no doubt, some initial words of instruction. It is not intended that she actually understand his words. She knows why the women around her are laughing hysterically; this is all so ridiculous, this long, tall drink of water doing push-ups, using the chair arms as support, bringing his face down to hers, then pulling it back up as his arms straighten—he's been in the military, he's carrying out orders, she's given the orders, fifty push-ups on the double, that sort of scenario, and it's in play before she can even pull it together enough to resist, before she can say, "No, really, militaristic domination is not my thing." Jesus, she thinks, not at all, and she starts to be disturbed by how the dancers are reading them. She can't turn her head to signal for help before the dancer's face is once again in hers. The room is smoky, but she can smell him, soap and water and a unisex scent from one of the corporate clothing stores, J. Crew or Banana Republic, not an over-powering men's cologne, and not floral. "I could be your mother," she says to him, and just as quickly realizes the bizarre attempt at shaming him that that comment is, but in his eyes is a look of interest, and once again the affection she has been observing ever since they arrived. She wonders what his childhood had been like, this young male beauty. He couldn't have had a particularly happy one if he'd washed up on these shoals—not necessarily her thighs, she doesn't mean that, but this entire shabby enterprise of enticement. Fine by me that you could be my mother his eyes say, gladdening, all the better his eyes say, *we're not exactly invested in doing things the usual way here.* And as he raises himself, she turns, in time to see a look of unchecked disgust in her partner's eyes, and the dancer, as attuned to a vibe as anyone can possibly be, springs up and away and is as briskly somewhere else as he was initially so briskly doing push-ups on the arms of her chair. "Whenever . . ." he drones slowly over his shoulder, "you just signal." Lose the ball and chain, his flattened inflection says, lose the breeder.

She laughs, and as she's laughing she knows this may be a fatal error, to laugh, and yet, what isn't risible here? She's come by his behest to a strip club in Vegas. . . . Of course, she realizes, of course her willingness may be her fatal error, her laughing willingness. The tall dancer turns his face back over his shoulder, fixes her with his flashing eyes, and calls—his voice lilting into the din—words she can't distinguish, isn't—once again—supposed to.

"Anyone else you want to bring down upon your-self?" he asks with good humor, as deft a revision of the earlier disgust in his eyes as he can manage. And he *is* deft, smart, appalled at himself. *Can't help it*, he might be think-ing. *Don't mean it*, he might be insisting. *I love you*, he might be pleading. "That one over there isn't bad," and he nods his chin at a tightly wound blond dancer about to swing up onstage.

"You a small piece of leather, but you well put together," a busboy used to say to her, and this dancer is precisely that as he gazes at the floor, smoothing violet fringe down along the legs of his ultra-suede chaps. His hair has fallen into his eyes, where he leaves it, looks out through it across the stage, a brattiness in his face she couldn't like, couldn't be attracted to. He reaches up and tweaks his nipples viciously, licks the palm of one hand, getting into it, the palm of the other, then slaps his naked buttocks—bare haunches. "Yee haw! Let's ride! It's Show-time—let the nipples be erect!" And he's up onstage, pur-ple fringe flying, a red imprint of his hand on one cheek; he's leaning over, sassing the audience with his ass, and then he twitches the other cheek at the audience and it too is emblazoned with the angry red imprint of a hand.

Violet Chaps is a different show than the boys before. He's all about himself, and he does his dance churning deeper and deeper into himself—no woman is brought onstage—he is there for viewing, and then the chaps go fly-ing and beneath the nylon or Qiana thong his penis is full long, adamantine beneath its thin sheath, and the room begins to change.

Tattoo

❖

The young woman is almost past the window of Restaurant Tanuki. A small curiosity stops her and she leans toward the glass to peer in at the chefs behind the sushi counter preparing for the evening. One slices octopus tentacle with brisk, adroit draws of his knife, as though performing a martial exercise. She can see the rouged suckers along the length of the tentacle, can see this curious surface entire even after the tentacle is disks of white, white meat serried along the wooden counter. The sushi chef's head is bowed, concentrating, and she stares at the life-size tattoo of a sinewy arm reaching up his neck beneath his earlobe and deep into his hairline, where surely tattoo fingers hold something, a peach or a saber, perhaps merely the globe of the chef's head, as though he were an infant in the hands of a dark-skinned god. But beneath the chef's black hair the inky fingers of the tattoo are a mystery, what they hold, how they hold it, whether the wrist of the tattoo even articulates into fingers or not. Though of course the wrist does, she knows it does, because one evening while she was sitting at the sushi bar, he turned just enough, and in the way sunlight angled just right reveals black spots on a black leopard, she could see the beginning of dark fingers beneath black hair, could see the tattoo's continued anatomy—could not see much else, though, as he turned back with the leaden flesh of a salmon fillet draped between his palms.

Now, as his knife draws through the last pink curl of tentacle, he looks up: He knows someone is there. His quiet, stationary alertness seems intricately striated within his muscles; this is also martial. She pulls back from the window, from her small breathy fog on the glass broadening into his white T-shirt—he is there so suddenly, staring out at her, the tattoo arm emerging up from the crew neck of his white, white shirt, over the gully of his throat, past the earlobe, the great inky hand grasping his head like a shotput and driving it through the solid clear water of the window, a thousand sinewy arms refracting in the great splash of glass, a thousand ogre-ed faces, because her humiliation can so quietly, violently transmogrify, though he is only smiling wryly at her, his nostrils pressed up humorously against the shimmering glass.

She could not begin to tell you from whence the angry pistons of her heart, but she is furious pounding her way down the street, the sun firing one shop window after another so that on each silvered plane there swelters only a tin wilderness and no reflection of herself, nothing that might torque her outward for just an instant, make her see caught-in-the-act-of-staring as a silly sweet moment deserving laughter, goofy hiccup, bemused confession.

Instead, there pulses in her loud as a bugle a thousand regenerate moments of early shame, her father's joke year after year till she got it: "How do you get down from an elephant?" "You don't. You get down from a goose."

So many years to understand the joke, and then so many other instances. So many years the bitter discount of her father's derisive laugh—that indelible tattoo in her ears.

Pink

❖

Within the museum's permanent collection, another collection, and so small a subset, its entirety takes up a room no grander than a kitchen—and something accurate in this, as it is a room of cups and saucers. "Art of the Cup: A History of Design 1860–1960." The room is nestled at the back of the museum like a tiny almost vestigial organ amid great lungs and systolic heart, amid Greek Antiquities, Italian Renaissance, Colonial America. She can find this room blindfolded, in the dark, and the room itself is a little dark, though roseate, too, and the young woman loves drawing her friends into its closeness, their chuckles at the cup shaped like a dice on a saucer of porcelain playing cards, a spry red devil for a cup handle. They marvel politely—marvel only because she is herself marveling excitedly—at the cup in the shape of a French champagne cork on a bistro *l'addition* saucer; they murmur appreciatively, though only mildly so, at the slick, angular example of German moderne, at the unabashedly bosom-y French

Belle Epoque cup with its dragonfly handle. But there is always a high, unbidden amusement at one display, and she feels their immediate and compelling *comfort* upon seeing the Fiestaware cup, the diner china so familiar, so quotidian, they cannot help but laugh, and point, of course *point*. This cup takes dominion everywhere, she thinks, disappointed; it's so American, produced in staggering quantities in aggressively ingenuous colors, Cobalt, Chartreuse, Persimmon.

But she herself likes that just yesterday, the new Betty Crocker catalog came—Fiestaware, its blowsy colors soliciting across several pages, and even less expensive with points cut from Bisquick boxes or cake mixes. The design of this very same cup before her now in the museum can be had for ten dollars and forty-eight cents, indeed for five dollars and seventy-four cents if one has twenty-five points to throw at the transaction. Sometimes she regales her friends with this information, makes them laugh by suggesting a little more baking on their part, a return to stick-to-your-ribs flapjacks, and they too can own something valued by a curator.

Her friends glance at one or two more cups as they leave, the Italian demitasse or the regal Austrian chocolate cup, and then she is once again standing here alone, listening to their footsteps enter Arts and Crafts Movement in Great Britain and America.

She knows a poet, Molly, who ventures that the greatest sentence in the English language just might be the one spoken dozens of times a day at the Disneyland ride: "Please wait 'til your teacup has come to a complete stop." So, always, the young woman thinks to say to her friends, "You have *not* waited. You have not given this room enough time. I have so much to tell you. . . ." But she never holds them;

in fact, she motions them on, her hands and face conveying that she will join them in time; she understands their interest is minor, understands also that the intimacy of this room makes them uncomfortable and that they do not know why.

She moves from a Faïence d'Art cup with a fanciful earthenware lip folded in and fluted out to a pink cup of porcelain almost translucent and in the shape of a cactus flower. She loves this cup's pink, how very pretty it is, the pink of peonies, sweet pea, lisianthus. She has grown tired of being at baby showers for little girls in which ebullient, relieved appreciation is heaped at clothes that are black or green or yellow, the "Thank God! No pink!" reaction; she is tired of this misogyny, this judgment that is somehow not judgment because somehow in the moment it is taste or style, even, unbelievably, social progress. She loves this pink, and in the shape of a flower. "Flowers are genitals," her friend Julia had said once. "That's why we give them to our lovers."

If he were here ever, or now, standing beside her, she would tell him how she had learned the expression "shows pink" many years ago, from a young man who relished telling her and whom she relished remembering. His name was Brian, and somehow they had gotten on the subject of *Hustler* and *Playboy* magazines and the phrase "shows pink"—or rather, "does not show pink" came into the conversation, and she had stopped him and then laughed, getting it, though not before he'd seen that it was news for her, this phrase, its meaning. *Playboy* magazine does not show pink, the inner roseate folds of the labia minora, and though technically and within the trade this is true, the blushy soft porcelainized photography seems to her forthrightly labial, as does the lighting of this room in the museum.

This room *shows pink* she would say to him were he standing here beside her now, her finger on the glass before the translucent pink cactus flower cup. She would say this, laughingly, to say much more.

If he were here now she would tell him about the word porcelain, the word coming from the Latin, *porcellus,*

little pig, vulva,

which was—she felt sure of it—

an affectionate term for the female vulva, *porcellina!* those beautiful translucent pinks, labial, suckling, piglet, shoat, sweet in one sense, *porcellina,* an early version of La Chatte, or pussy—porcellina, little pig!

. . . less sweet, certainly, in another sense of livestock, chattel. But she can love the pink of pork, of ham, of pro-sciutto di Parma, can see this spectrum as labial, sexual, can savor prosciutto wrapped around effusively vaginal figs—or *fica,* the current Italian word for female genitalia.

If he were here now, she would tell him the word *por-cellana* in Italian means "cowrie shell" and derives also from *porcello,* "little pig," "vulva," because of the shell's resemblance to female pudenda, a resemblance evincing itself in two ways, the cloven vaginal cleft and the shell's beautiful porcelain surface speckled brown and taupe and blushing pink near its opening, near its *introitus,* the Latin for vaginal opening, the word *introit* being also the psalm sung at the beginning of an Anglican service or of a Mass—the entering in.

She liked cathedrals better this way, liked churches better this way—as an entering into herself, into a circuitry of reproduction, not a system of birth or production, but of *re*production, the seeds in the dark ovarian caves, dropping one here, one there, a constancy of possibility happening and happening and happening—like ocean tide, that hydrolic loyalty grinding cowrie shells, all those little vulvae, until they were sand, were clay, were taken up newly plastic and made into porcelain shapes and fired, become teacups, become the intimacy of lips, of his lips upon her own. She would tell him all this.

She thinks of dying sometimes, of a last will and testament, of cremation, the bone ash of her incinerated body mixed with kaolin, china stone, silicate, lime—oh, what potter would take on this commission for a lonely man? And yet, Why Not? his lover set upon the table, tea set, chocolate set, coffee set, why not lips upon her always, his tongue against the thin bone china lips her fired bones would make? When he kisses porcelain, he kisses cowrie shell, vulva, little pig, pink, bones, her. Why not begin every morning entering her?

Behold, I make all things new, this room of cups no bigger than a kitchen.

Place

❖

Narthex is the word she keeps repeating to herself, *narthex*, but she knows this is not the right word for where the congregants sit, for where she sits now amid the empty pews and the huge speakers buzzing from the aisles, amplifying their presence and nothing more. Blessedly nothing more, she thinks, eyeing the drum set and the two electrical guitars where an altar might be, and the electrified double bass leaning up against the choir box.

What has she gotten herself into, driving to Beverly Hills for a 6:00 P.M. Saturday evening service at All Saints? What has she bathed and dressed for, black suit and black pearls and black shoes and bag? What is she looking for?

Nothing she could have predicted by what she gazes upon now, the forty or so people gathered here, not enough bodies to fill up even an eighth of the sanctuary, or to fill up whatever it is that this part of a church is called—transept?—and though most of them sit forward, gathered to the left side in the front pews, she is not the only solitary woman in the more shadowy reaches of the church at 6:00 P.M. She doesn't turn around to take a count, to poll these stark faces too much like her own, some hunger writ huge across the eyes and cheekbones—she doesn't turn to see what she could draw had she ability with charcoal or ink. But she knows she can't be the only woman come out on a Saturday night seeking respite.

What had he said to her, her former colleague, the Ezra Pound scholar, what was it that he had so gleefully proposed a year after her husband's death? *That it must really be rather exciting to be able to completely redesign your life now!*

And now it is two years after his death to the day, January 7, and once again a Saturday night, and then it comes to her, *nave*, yes, *nave*, that is the word for this part of the church, and then her mind nudges the word, nudges the homophone, knave, the jack in cards, *knave*, is that what she is in search of? A knave? But no, even if she assumes—and she does—that a 6:00 P.M. Saturday evening service will necessarily attract single people, particularly single women not inclined to bars or gyms, she has not come for a church-imprimatured singles service.

At the front of the church—from the *sacristy*—the musicians file in, followed by a young blonde woman in jeans and a knit cap who takes up the standing mike and welcomes what seems primarily a gathering of the congregation's young, all friends, it appears, the 6:00 P.M. Saturday evening service no doubt their idea, their insistence, "Not our grandparents' church," they might have argued to the church elders, "we need something else, services that meet our needs and attend to our issues and speak our language."

The musicians ready themselves onstage, the guitarists and bass player; they lean down to plug in cords, to turn knobs; they straighten up to adjust straps. Their tennis shoes, their knit hats, their sweatshirts—it all glares to her in the overly bright track lighting suspended from the high ceiling, and then the drummer ambles in, tapping his sticks against the worn knees of his cords.

The song the young blonde woman opens with—would one use this language in a church, she wonders, "opening act," "opens with"?—is not gospel or hymn; in fact, it is, to her ears, so bland a musical offering, it falls to the category "female recording artist," but the young blonde woman sings and the sound is plaintive enough and lovely enough and *just* enough and not much more, and this is all what it is supposed to be, she realizes, inoffensive, mild, yes, almost unbearably inoffensive, but far more important, the 6:00 P.M. Saturday evening service is the result of the young of the congregation having been heard, having gotten their own forum. . . .

Were she at home now, in bed, her eyes closed, she would take herself to Certosa, to the monastery high above Florence—she would walk up the hill to it, and then she would walk within its walls, the famous Della Robbias lining the inner courtyard, the raised ceramic saints and Madonnas and angels in their white robes against the sky blue enamel, there since the fifteenth century in the tremendous quiet beauty of this monastery of an order of silent monks, each with his own apartment, and each apartment with its own garden. When she does this, when she takes herself to Certosa, she imagines her body curled in the narrow monk's bed, knees to chin, her own irrefutable geography, but she sees the blood of her futile heart seeping out over her chest and arms and legs, flooding across the rough wooden floor, down the narrow wooden stairs and out into the old soil of the garden. No roses, no, she does not even ask to make roses, just dissolution; most any night she asks just for that.

Usually, on Saturday evenings, she goes to her Korean spa. She sits in the whirlpool alone in the dim lighting, her face turned to the glass-brick wall, steam or tears or sweat, no matter, the busy lights of a busy city street below, each car an abstract penumbra within which, she resolves, there are people going somewhere, people with lives, and in contradistinction to her heart, she feels happy for them; she urges them on to dinner tables and movie theaters and even brawls and spats and screaming arguments—any scenario in which those they love are alive.

She pays to have her body touched, a scrub, an oil massage, the Korean women always very sweet to her. They think she looks like Julie Andrews, "Yes, yes, Julie Andrew, just like her, very nice," and they seem so amused by this idea that it amuses her, their amusement, but sometimes she will be so lost beneath their touch, vigorous as it is, and then she will feel a face close to her own, and she will feel a little tap on her shoulder, so light a tap, timid, polite, and she will struggle up through the many layers of subdued self to find a smiling face, saying, "Julie Andrew, look just like her, Julie Andrew" . . . and let alone what do you do with a problem like Maria, what do you do with a perception like this? The primary author of this idea calls herself "Jackie," but of course she has a Korean name, and the woman thinks that probably "Jackie" is as disparate from who she is as Julie Andrews is from her, but she has a form of love for these women, who do not know her with any particularity of character, but who care for her and have cared for her with no small degree of attention, even affection.

Once, maybe six weeks after he had died, and her sister had left and the house was empty, she sat at the spa in a white plastic chair, waiting for a massage, and Tina, who didn't give scrubs or massages, came from behind the desk and draped a towel over her bare shoulders. Tina knew nothing and somehow everything she needed to know, and she had taken a small white towel and pulled its rough ends around her neck and looked down at her and quietly walked away. It wasn't a moment that could possibly mean anything to anyone else, other than it was a moment that pulled the human animal back into the fold—a moment that said there were a few in this species who didn't shame you with their violence. . . .

A man stands from the front pew and he takes the microphone from the singer and he thanks her and greets "those gathered here" and exhorts them all to stand and to sing in praise of God. There are no programs, and if the hymns are listed somewhere, she can't find the board. She is not the only person who doesn't sing, who doesn't know what to sing, and the sound coming from the congregants is subdued, if not desultory. In the middle of the second song, she sits down, too tired to pretend any longer, and interestingly enough, it draws a disapproving look from the young man who is presiding, and she wonders—is amazed really—that the puerile affectation of his jeans and tennies and untucked shirt are seemingly not in question, but a well-dressed forty-nine-year-old woman sitting down and quietly crossing her legs during this self-styled praising of the Lord is? The tyranny of hip, she decides, against the tyranny of depression.

She knows she has come to All Saints in Beverly Hills in search of quiet, cloister . . . and perhaps she has come in search of formality . . . almost *any* formality . . . the conventions within which she can abide for a time. "After great pain, a formal feeling comes—" She hears Dickinson's pentameter in her head, the five beautiful feet, and then she hears her before she sees her, the hurried tattoo of heels down the center aisle becoming a small woman in tight jeans tucked into boots and hunching in a rabbit-fur jacket. She dips quickly as she genuflects and sits down two pews from the front. Her hair color is what the woman has come to think of as bright Russian blonde, and the hair is dry and stiff, and the glimpse she catches is of a sunken face hung with make-up, the way a woman's face looks after it has been beaten over a long period of time, the bones liquified beneath, the flesh lumpy and sallow and inert. She appears to be what the woman's mother good-naturedly called "local talent," but this is Beverly Hills, and if she is local talent, she is not charging much these days. Within two minutes her cell phone goes off and she hastens down the empty pew and out along the far aisle, rabbit fur and spangles and the warren-like curvature of her back and the hard pounding of boot heels, and within this cameo playing out before her, within the nasty technological jangle scoring it, she now sees clearly the woman's destroyed face—sees it as though it is some form of cautionary mirror.

She is defined now almost completely by negation, by what she is no longer, by what she cannot have, by absence, and most pointedly by a toxic physiology she would transfuse into almost anything else.

In December, her graduate students had been so taken with a description in one of their stories, a lot of "yeah"s around the workshop table, a few admiring "so perfect, man,"s and she had grown quiet within their excitement. Some battles she sat back from, though probably she wasn't known for that. "A forty-year-old face on an eighteen-year-old body." They knew exactly what that was, perfect, man, perfect, and their sense of the "authenticity" of that description, that phenomenon they all had seen, puzzled at, and—it inflected their voices so subtly—the offense they took at this unnaturalness.

The mildest way she could have gone about it in workshop, she realizes now, is to have asked quietly why the average age for girls starting to menstruate was now approaching ten years of age, when thirteen used to be the norm . . . and in America in the seventeenth century menarche occurred around the age of eighteen. She had it on good word that the female of the species needed about eighty thousand calories on board to trigger ovulation, and girls were just fatter now. She didn't know about eighteen-year-old bodies owning thinness, nor what a forty-year-old body was versus an eighteen-year-old body. Oh yeah, sure, she knew, but what was far more common these days—

should she wish to traffic in stereotypes—was eighteen-year-old faces on forty-year-old bodies.

But why, really, hadn't she touched the comment in workshop? Why had she given their volley of adulation time? It was a description of a waitress, she thinks, but she doesn't remember for sure. She remembers the inflection in their voices, hears it in her head when occasionally she turns around and finds someone looking at her, their eyes very quickly slicing away, disappearing her, she is older than they had thought, history there in the face that they might have to accommodate. Better to run in the opposite direction. She agrees. She doesn't want them anywhere near how shattered she is. Eighteen years is how long she lived with him; forty years could be what is left of her life—her body within this life—and she does not think she is up for this physical wilderness.

The man freehands his talk, which is about his job in the movie industry and his disenfranchisement, his young marriage and children and the return of his own abusive childhood to haunt him and render him incapable of work, of raising his children lovingly, and he talks on, and what might better be the content of a heart-to-heart with one's closest friend—or a therapist's session—is nonetheless offered as testimony to his God's fine and wise machinations in his life. He mentions twice the patience of his young and loving wife, and the woman thinks the wife more deserving of praise than this dottering mythology, but then she had gotten herself here, hadn't she, had gotten herself dressed and up and out of the house on a Saturday night and plunked her respectfully dressed self down within these vestiges?

* * *

Three banners suspended by macramé hang from the tall ceilings, a flowing white dove against teal felt, a brown cross against red, and a gold crosier beneath a single silver star whose points have become unglued and flop like ears, a funny, unintentional way, she supposes, of suggesting sheep, a flock. She is reminded of how much as a child she liked the way felt cutouts stuck to a felt board, letters and numbers, or all the colored animals doubling their way up to Noah's ark, the soft magic of their staying in place.

Lauren comes to see her at school and shows her a story she has written about working on a horse farm in Wales. There is the detail of the dead foal, its body being left with the mother in the paddock, the best way for the mare to get over her foal's death, the best way for the mare to grieve. (She assumes there is something hormonal at work here, too, the involution of the mare's womb triggered perhaps by her smelling her foal? She doesn't know.)

At home, away from school, she sleeps curled around a large leather book the size of a big dictionary or a family Bible. It contains his ashes. This is how she goes to sleep now, her hand reached across, touching the brown leather, the way she slept always touching him, her arm hooked in his. She can't imagine his remains anywhere else but where he slept beside her when he was alive—can't imagine anyone prescribing this as salutary, but there were months of nights she slept curled into a ball, keening like an animal, her chest heaving with desire. This is better.

For all her culture's attention to the physical, it seemingly has little to salve the creatural anguish of losing someone else's body, their touch, their heat, their oceanic heart. "Are you dating yet?" In other words, get another body, and practically speaking, that is practical, logistical, but she doesn't want another body, she wants the body she loved, the forceps scar across his cheek that she traced with her hand, his penis, its elegant sweep to the side, the preternaturally soft skin. One wants what one has loved, not the idea of love. His ashes within a brown leather book are better than ideas.

She acknowledges the superior intellectual position of being a radical epistemological skeptic—how can you really know anything at all?—but intuitively, emotionally, calling herself agnostic suggests a pack of lies she can't reside within, most particularly the idea that perhaps creatures don't die, or perhaps certain creatures don't die—because God knows, He's an epicurean bastard picking and choosing with his silver fork—and the one aspect of her life that she is in profound knowledge of is cessation, death. She thinks that probably no matter what religion one draws up around oneself within, the dead are not hysterically funny; they don't make you laugh; the dead do not record themselves reading *Swann's Way* to you, or eat with you or sneeze, or make love to you; the dead are not so deeply inside you, hurting you, the way he did sometimes because he liked to be so physically there; the dead do not pour out of you across your thighs. She is not agnostic; she knows what she knows. She hasn't come to meet others who believe as she believes, hasn't come thinking the aegis of Episcopalianism means anything at all . . . nor has she come to make fun of any mythology by which the human animal makes sense of pain.

* * *

She looks back up at the high ceiling hung with felt banners. She makes a point these days of looking up. It's a trick her friend Leslie taught her, that her father, the psychologist, taught her, that looking up, perceiving with the head tilted back, actually entails a different part of the brain and is good for depression. Because she refuses to take anti-depressants, she hears Leslie's voice instructing her, and she struggles to look up on her walks, to read all the billboards, to count air conditioners on rooftops, or solar panels or pigeons or the ricketry of antennae, but then she is mostly looking down again, particularly when someone is looking at her; she looks down or to the side, tries to walk very quickly so that no one will stop her, will catch her eye, will approach her, as this only adds to the depression. Yes, of course she's doing fine, yes, of course, thank you for asking—all the decorum deployed to keep her in the functioning, legitimate exchange of the world.

What would her friends think of her if they knew that she would bargain their lives to have him back, would sanction their slaughter could he walk through the door from the garden, his arms thrown up, laughing, the way he came home, "Hey, it's me, I'm home," the beautiful silly irony of that statement? What would they think of the violence of her mind now, how it worked over and over the ancient abacus: *If I did this for you, God, if I believed you existed, would you do this for me?* If she made this pact with the Devil—for surely God and the Devil were one, big pals, inseparable—was that why she was sitting in a church on a Saturday night? Had she gone to His house for some plain reckoning? But then again, that's what the Book of Job was about to her, a cautionary tale about wanting there to be a God, wanting there to be someone who could enact what a God could enact, or who could sanction what the Devil would do. You want this, people? You want these kinds of powers? No, you don't, and here's why, and here's why it's sheer vanity to want them in any other entity. Look what sort of violence would rain down. Poor Job, sure, poor Job with his hives and his financial losses—though who needs three thousand camels?—and too bad about the kids, forgive me, they were delicious, so sweet and so cold, sure, too bad, but it's God who's the miserable bastard here. Look what he got himself up to! No good could come of that type of power; that's what the writer of the Book of Job was saying, and she knew the writer was right.

The young man is now instructing them to write down on a piece of paper their problem, the problem they need to solve, the problem most pressing in on their happiness. They are all going to drop this jotting down into a huge hammered brass bowl that the young man has produced from the front pew. The bowl looks African to her, or perhaps Indian, something a cobra could easily curl within; it also looks like a larger version of the vessel that the last emperor of China defecates into and which his doctors sniff diagnostically, rolling the stools around in order not to miss any pernicious element, and then sniffing again. It is an amazing scene, a throwaway almost, and yet visceral in a way that movies rarely are. She has always remembered it . . . but she doesn't think the young man is quite up to that sort of thing appearing in this bowl. She thinks of her great-grandmother's wisdom imparted to her, something she was instructed always to remember, from the time she was a little girl, and she had remembered, and she had believed it, though after his death it took her a few months to return to it, to find it true once again. Her great-grandmother said—she could hear her saying it—if everyone sat around a table and put their problems in the middle of that table, they would all end up taking their own problems back.

She gathers the two black leather handles of her purse and rises swiftly and scoots from the pew and walks quickly down the center aisle. A woman seated several pews behind her looks up at her leaving, and the look is desperate, a look that says, Please take me with you. The woman's pale brown hair hangs straight to her shoulders and the woman seems somehow biblical, veiled, and she does think to lean down and say "Let's go, come on, let's get out of here," but she doesn't have a thing she can offer the woman that she doesn't desperately need herself, and anyway, where could they go.

The Moon

※

The young woman sees the moon tonight has paused behind a cloud. With only the light from the hall, the dining room, as her grandmother likes it, is dim. She watches her grandmother spoon soup from an old aluminum pan tilting on its warped bottom, the handle pitching upward at an odd angle. Beneath the pan are the violet threads of a crocheted pot holder, and beneath the pot holder is the white lace cloth of her grandmother's dining room table.

The pan, canted crazily, rocks on the crocheted pot holder as her grandmother moves her spoon into the clear broth and out again, as though a small vacuum were created with each spoonful removed, a tiny suck that pulls the pan forward and then, giving out, allows the pan back again.

The young woman watches the pan seesaw on this fulcrum, this bulging warp of aluminum, and remembers how in this very house, as children, she and her brother pushed the breakfast-nook table back and forth between them within the horseshoe banquette. Who could pin whom between table and upholstered back? Who could tip whose cereal bowl, or—the breakfast-nook table pitching suddenly!—make the other snort their milk in shock?

At the back of the house and just off the kitchen, the breakfast nook in the evenings was a galley, a Wynken, Blynken, and Nod set off to sea in a wooden shoe, and their grandmother often sat there with them, straight-backed and merry, a mid-night snack of cheese and crackers and cocoa—"'Where are you going, and what do you wish?' the old moon asked the three"—but she is now so bowed, she cannot fit within the booth—so involutional, she is the horseshoe shape of the banquette itself—but with each spoonful of broth at the dining room table, the pan rocks like a sabot on the waves. . . .

Crazy

The students were thanking her and then hugging her, filing out the front door and leaving down the walk. They liked the food, the wheat berry salad and the fennel tart. They liked the beer, too, and would she go with him to school sometime to hear a reading of one of their plays, or a rehearsal, perhaps have lunch with them? Polite. The students were always so polite to her, and funny; they made jokes about him that amused her. Of course, they were drama students, and so they were lively and performative, joyfully outrageous, on fire. Did she know that he talked about her in rehearsals, said, "I defer to my wife on this. . . ." One young woman—she stood so tall—said, "You're his example for almost anything having to do with women." The young woman smiled and it was genuine, her ink-blue eyes glistening; she was the talent in the group, Benson said, "It's too bad she's so tall."

"Now we know why," said another young woman,

and it took her a moment to realize this was a compliment to her, that they understood why she was a measure of womanhood or homemaking or cooking. It referred to so much, this compliment, and she knew they were taking their notes here, now, in her home, their home, Benson's and hers. It made her nervous most times having them here, so many sets of avid eyes. Some of it was sweet attention, the fact that they were at school and away from real homes, stable living situations with full batteries of pots and pans. They hadn't seen a four-square meal in days, nor cloth napkins and glasses that matched. They wandered the house, looking at the paintings, or playing with the wicket in the front door, this bit of theatrical business, and today Benson had even directed them into their bedroom—really into their walk-in closet—to look at the original Playbills from Odets's *Clash by Night* and Eugene O'Neill's *The Iceman Cometh*. So many of them had stood in their bedroom, but one of the young men had plunked down on the bed, drinking his beer, one of his knees hiked up, with his boot heel on the bed rail. It's just a length of wood, she said to herself, and his boot heel will do no damage. It was an old, old bed, one that she had brought to the marriage, a spool bed inherited from her Southern aunt. They were reproducing them now, though this was an original from Louisiana, from the 1870s, and made of West Indian mahoghany. She hadn't wanted it to be their bed, their marriage bed; it had seemed too grandmotherly, and Benson stretched its entire length and then some, but they had been as poor as these graduate students were now, and had been happy to even have a bed. A small white panel truck delivered it to their New York apartment all the way from Shreveport, the men calling ahead to make sure someone was there in the three-story walk-up to receive it. On the busy, filthy sidewalk when the moving blankets dropped from the turned rungs of the bed's footboard, a check, secured on one end with Scotch tape, stood up like a playing card clothespinned to a bicycle spoke. On the back of the check was scrawled "Buy yourself a good mattress and box spring, one which will take a lot of action! Love Tante Çéçé." She hadn't loved the suggestion of her aunt's note—it embarrassed her—and even worse was the absurd amount, enough for five mattress sets. She worried that these moving men had read her aunt's ornate scrawl, had laughed their way up the Eastern Seaboard, and when Benson came striding down the street, waving, his face alight, he and the men laughed and she heard the words "We brought the launchpad to the rocket," and the deep male laughter, and she watched from the window the vigorous handshakes and Benson putting money in their hands. "My aunt already paid them," she said when Benson came up the stairs and in the front door. "She tipped them, too. You didn't need to give them money."

"Oh, why not," Benson had said. "They're in New York City. They need to play a bit." She had felt mean, a check for five thousand dollars in her hand and she stood there begrudging these men a little mad money.

Of course, she and Benson bought a very fine mattress and box spring, and because of this had used the bed for so long, it became their bed, and then, even longer into the years, after they had replaced that initial mattress set, it would have meant something too ominous to have changed out the bed frame . . . and then what would the preferred bed have been anyway? "I can't hear you for this goddamn bed," Benson complained, its squeaking and moaning quickening over the years as the different climates dried out the old wood. Or Benson would ask, amused, "Is that you or the bed?" or he would ask, his lips against her ear, "Was it as good for you as it was for the bed?" But Benson loved Tante Çéçé and would not have hurt her for the world, even if she might never have found out about them purchasing something new and less rickety. It was just something Benson wouldn't do in the world, and of course she had always agreed, had loved this observance in him.

But this summer, in the dense, unnerving heat, Benson moved her against the wall and ran his hands up under her wet arms and then up around her sticky neck. "Stop," she pleaded, "stop. I'm a sweaty mess." But he wouldn't, and he turned and pressed her into the bed and said, "I don't care—you think I care about sweat. I want my mouth on you." That was his expression, he wanted his mouth on her, but she could not understand this desire, could not imagine allowing anything so disgusting. "No," she said, pushing his head from between her legs. "No. Why must you want this so much?"

He jerked his face away from her hand. "Why indeed," he said, and then he shifted his weight and rolled away, and she raised her head, to see him licking the mahoghany rungs of the footboard, "chewing the scenery," a phrase she knew from him. And then she said as much: "You're chewing the scenery."

Now she shook the young man's hand who had sat on the bed, the bed that had strangely not made a peep. His hand felt grainy and thick and cold, but her hands were always too warm, clammy. "I've read your books," he said quietly. "They were helpful to my family."

Oh, she thought, his hand falling from hers. She was always surprised when someone knew that she had done something other than stand by Benson's side as he bade his students good-bye. It was not Benson who spilled the beans, and her *Oh* was in large measure her surprise that someone yet again had spoken about her, had identified her. What diligent soul in Benson's department took it upon himself?

"You have a little sister," she asked the young man, "or a sister, yes?"

"Yes," he said.

"She eats now?"

"Yes," he said again, "sort of," and then he was gone down the steps and she heard his boot heels against the brick, resonant and pronounced, the jostle of the buckles. She liked the way his black leather jacket hiked up his back. She could see his faded blue shirttail just coming untucked. She liked these students; she liked them all, their tremendous, vulnerable power. Then Benson had her by the shoulders from behind and pulled her into himself and kissed her on the top of the head. "I'll be right back in," he said, and because he was an actor and he knew how to breathe, how to enunciate and project, his words blew hot across her scalp, as though even before she saw what she was about to see, the fire had begun.

"Come along, Mercutio," Benson said, "that knuckle-head Romeo awaits your death." Benson's "talent," the tall Meagan, turned and smiled at her; she clutched her purse to her side, intoned what so many of them had intoned, thank-yous, appreciation, and then she passed out the door at Benson's insistence, his arms aloft, directing. The tall Meagan bowed awkwardly, a performance, stumbling into a funny drunken walk, and then she hung a moment on the iron gate, delivering lines:

"'No, 'tis not so deep as a well, nor so wide as a

church-door, but 'tis enough, 'twill serve. Ask for me to-morrow, and you shall find me a grave man. I am pep-per'd—'"

Benson laughed and pulled the front door shut.

Inside, it was so suddenly quiet, even the music was between tracks, and then slowly the deep sounds of Mingus fingering his bass. She stood looking at the door's panels and the iron wicket that rattled. She could open the little grille and look through, but she thought, No, don't. She walked into the front room and gathered glasses and napkins onto a tray. Two cashews remained in the nut bowl. They looked to her like huge commas, and she leaned down and plucked them from the bowl and ate them. Mercutio's lines—didn't they signal the turning point in the play, the comedy ending and the tragedy beginning? She moved to the front window and looked out. She thought the talent and Benson well matched. They stood talking, first Meagan's head down, with her hair falling forward, obscuring her face, and then his face down, and then her hands held behind her back and her lovely face tilted up to his. Benson knew an audience at his back when he had one, and he never touched her, never even leaned down to kiss her on the cheek—blameless—but this was how she, his wife in the window, knew. All theater people hugged and kissed all the time. They were crazy for it.

Involution

Walking—strolling—her reflection shoulder-to-shoulder with her, strolling in the windows, her partner, company, though sometimes as warning or surprise even, her shoulders more hunched than she liked, her grandmother's body curled so tightly in upon her lungs that she could not breathe enough to climb a flight of stairs, her bones so leached of calcium by babies that she became the nautilus shape herself, that trick of fetuses of taking over the body, of leaving an X-ray of themselves in their mothers forever, of leaving a shape their mothers can return to, of leaving the future behind even as they take it with them, of leaving in their mothers' bodies the idea of gestation, even very often of growth, the idea of metastasis, of cells galvanized, of disease given womb.

She—the young woman with very slightly hunched shoulders reflected in the shop windows—thought it surprising, too, that she looked thinner than the figure she had punished herself for earlier, in other words, better than

she'd assumed, good enough even for her to take her vitamins and calcium supplements that evening, though she
knew they made her gain weight, jumped her body into
some unnaturally warm gear she didn't know how to cool,
how to control. What she loved about being thin, about
her body without supplements or vitamins, was that her
body was cold, and was, because of that, her own; what she
loved about other people was that their bodies were warm,
at least warmer than hers, certainly their hands and feet,
certainly their noses.

In bed, in sex, her feet and legs marble, she could
chart the physiology of reproduction, could account for the
hugely various temperatures of her body by reasoning out
what the fetus, were there one in her uterus, were there one
about to be in her uterus, would want, or need—desire and
necessity being one at that point. Warmth, heat, the sun
high within her abdomen, calories—all concentrated there
for one purpose only. But her feet were her own, were left
to her, were freezing, and in those moments they could fall
off and she wouldn't notice.

Her shoulder passed through the gold lettering on
the shop window where she bought chocolates for her
friends who ate chocolates, Amy and John, who liked those
god-awful American truffles that were almost as big as
trumpet mutes and had the unfortunate shape of a suppos-
itory, though, granted, they were squatter, not so much a
tiny missile as the nose of a bigger missile. She waved
through the glass at Eileen, beautiful white-haired Eileen
with a decorum almost decadent, almost French, and then
out of the corner of her eye she saw at the cross street, in
the cross street, a child, a toddler, that unmistakable size,
and a car starting across the intersection, starting to dart
because of traffic, and she bolted the ten yards to the curb

and off the curb, feeling the impact of the leap in her knees, feeling the tiny palm touch her palm, the palm stiff and smooth, pulling the child up above her, above her head so it was away, feeling the long stiff smooth bludgeon of the car bumper as it struck her thighs and knees, feeling something wrong, very wrong, the car, its impact right, the child too weightless, too stiff, landing too lightly, and someone standing on the corner, laughing, laughing, "It was a doll," the person giggling, "a doll," the car tire rolling across the young woman's legs, the bones cracking like a glass shattered at a Jewish wedding, and the second tire, the back tire, rolling across what now made a very different sound, the bones returned to meat.

The reflection of her inside shoulder just grazed the bottom of the gold lettering across the chocolate shop's window, *Confections in Chocolate*, though her shoulder, its reflection brushed first the word *Chocolate*, its *e* and *t* and *l*, and then the word *in* and then *Confections*, her shoulder, its reflection, reading exactly the way her eye did when she stood inside the shop looking out into the street, the color of cars and of people's clothing filling in the letters, behind her the sound of Eileen filling a box with chocolates from the vitrine, the crackling paper of the brown fluted cups as they were lifted and slid across cardboard, the muted whiz of cars passing in the street. Inside the shop, reading etalocohC, the word looked so much more like the Aztec *xocolatl*, from which the word *chocolate* derived; this amused her. She told no one what her shoulders knew. So little mattered enough to tell—etalocohC ni snoitcefnoC—if you know what I mean, she said to herself, to no one, pronouncing in her mind etalocohc ni snoitcefnoc perfectly, surprisingly perfectly—if you know what I mean. She laughed, raising her hand to wave to Eileen between the *c* of *Confections* and the long aluminum vertical of the doorjamb.

The good light that threw her body like a hologram on shop windows also made something glint up the street, a car's windshield, a side mirror, some instantly foiled surface, and in the tinseled diversion, in the turn of her eyes, a child in the cross street scuttling to her feet, the tiny bulkily padded rump raised like the hind end of some pastel beetle, and toward this child, toward this concentrated struggle, a car starting across the intersection, a fine black car now darting because of traffic, the light giving it all to the young woman as she, too, darted for the curb and off the curb, the stridency of the car's brakes just beginning as its fine glossy hood dipped like a grand piano lid being lowered. Then there was a very quiet, very muted sound, one of breaking, and the young woman looked at the shattered face up against the inside of the windshield, the bisque shards sliding down the glass, bouncing on the dashboard, and next to this the terrified face of a woman, her mouth open, her cheeks raised in fear, her eyes watching the little girl placing her hands on the curb, lifting her one leg and then the other, rising up from this stance to toddle down the sidewalk, her tiny shoe soles tapping away.

"What sort of a feckless mother are you?" the woman screamed at the young woman as she bolted from her car, and the young woman let her scream, let her scream and scream, and could not bring herself, nor any part of someone else she could muster, to defend herself, to tell the woman that the child was not hers, nor any child she knew. "I just got her from the hospital!" the woman screamed. "Just today, just now I got her!"

"From the doll hospital," the young woman said quietly, "is that what you mean, the doll hospital down the street?"

"What if I'd killed your little girl, killed her because you let her run in the street? What if I'd had to live with your incredible sadism? What sort of a life would I have? Are you that sick that you would do that to someone else's life?" and the woman sat back down in her car and reached across the seat and pulled the large headless doll to her chest, hugging it, a piece of the doll's neck pointing up into the woman's chin. It was a blade of bisque, a pale shark's tail swimming beneath a jutting rock.

They're marzipan," Eileen said. "I made them for this woman's wedding cake. The woman calls, says she wants dozens of tiny babies cascading down her cake. I love the idea. The cake is to be four tiers, and so I make two, almost three hundred of them, and I'm really proud of the color. I think I've gotten this perfect pink. She comes to pick them up to take them to her baker. She's the most beautiful black woman I've ever seen. I look at her, she looks at me, and, thank god, we both burst out laughing. She says she didn't even think to specify because she thought I'd just make them out of chocolate. I apologized and said I shouldn't have assumed. So I spent all that night making all these babies all over again, all in chocolate this time. Her brother comes early the next morning to get them and hands me this note. It says, 'Dear Eileen, please stick in a few pink ones. I want to freak out my new mother-in-law.'"

"What will you do with all these other babies?" the young woman asked. Eileen picked up a tray from the wide marble counter at the back of the shop. She walked the tray around the vitrine, out onto the floor. The tray was lined with truffles, fat American ones; atop each perched a tiny baby, a cupid or a Mercury, a cherub; each now had a fine set of wings, tiny, tiny wings that billowed out behind.

"And these are for the faint at heart," she said, walking back behind the case to exchange trays. This new tray had rows of truffles topped with babies, too. Three of these babies were fitted with scuba tanks, three with gas masks, three with tiny wristwatches and briefcases, three with computer keyboards in their laps; all the others were sprawled on their chocolate perches, pink chin in hand, their wings reaching out behind them, and they watched a television Eileen had made and stood in the center of the tray. Depicted on the tiny marzipan screen was a spraying tank, the kind used in an orchard or a garden. "Pesticide ad," she said, taking the tray back behind the vitrine.

"Ah," the young woman said, "I see." She thought about this, about confectioned chemicals. "So, how much for the TV babies? And for the TV, too, of course?"

"I don't know," Eileen responded. "Let me wrap it up for you first, get it ready to go."

"Yes, of course, whatever price."

The young woman left Confections in Chocolate with bigger and bigger boxes each time. This box now, this brood, rested in a box big enough for a cake. She held it with both hands, not by the thin white twine wound east and west and north and south, not by the knotted tangle at Four Corners; she held it like a ring bearer holding the pillow for the rings, held it that way as she went through the door onto the street.

She gasped, bolted forward, the box in her hands out of her hands as suddenly as she realized what was in the street was a lofted sheet of tissue paper, not what her brain

had so instantly viscerized it into, not what she was scrab-
bling for words to explain to the woman who had given
her—as they say—a wide berth, the woman who did not
lean down to help her retrieve her box of chocolates, the
woman who did not even stop a moment to hear her say "I
thought it was a child—in the street—a child. I saw it very
quickly, and it was everything a child could be, small and
supple and plump with new air." The woman's eyes were
full of disgust.

The young woman followed the other woman down
the street, followed not far behind, ticking off the items of
her clothing, "Ferragamo loafers, or perhaps old Ralph
Lauren, skirt Cacherel, ancient Cacherel, a good two or
three years old, scarf is not Hermès, not even Chanel; if
you're lucky it's Gucci, their cheapest, not even a hand-
stitched hem. Your purse is essentially an industrial-waste
product, though of course it's Fendi, who could miss the
distinctive *F*s." By this time a group of people had gathered
along the street, all looking at the woman as she scurried as
quickly as she could from the brands of her pursuer.

When the young woman stopped and turned back,
she saw that Eileen was kneeling down to pick up the tum-
bled box of chocolates, the hem of her white uniform
brushing the sidewalk. Eileen righted the box and then,
still kneeling, took a pair of scissors from her pocket and
snipped the quadrant of twine. The young woman watched
as the twine slithered down the sides of the box to the sidewalk. Eileen opened the box, pushing back the flaps, and
then stood and returned to her shop.

The young woman, when she approached, saw within the pink-walled box a ganglia of wings and tiny feet and
hands.

Caduceus

❖

It was too early to call to set an appointment, too early to deal with that office's feckless secretaries, too early to be in a bad mood, and now the kettle's harmonica whistle began to hum, giving the harpsicord picking out the beautiful Couperin some competition. Soon the kettle whistle would insist that she turn and walk to the stove and turn the gas off. "Okay then," she said to herself, "do this—you can do this." But she didn't.

She eyed the doctor's card propped at midnight against the coffee grinder so that she could not miss it as she made coffee in the morning—and now she was making coffee, or starting to, and it was bright out and the kettle mounted its pitch. She stood before the kitchen window holding the handset and did not turn to the stove.

She wished it were evening now, wished for the great relief of the calendar inking itself out, of day done and night coming, of ice cubes knocking about in a glass beneath the whiskey spilling in, that fine brown affirmation of need.

Instead, across the street the crepe myrtle shone livid in the sunlight, and the woman with the prodigious bosom walking her jounty French bulldog with a similar chest failed to amuse her . . . when always in the past, always. . . . Some mornings she called her sister in New York. "It's like they're both wearing torpedo bras—it's just the funniest sight," she'd told her.

Her heart was racing and she felt odd, jangly, chemical, everything in overdrive because of this radical thyroid she possessed. The doctor wanted to radiate it, but no, she didn't think she'd agree to that, or to drinking the radioactive isotope—that wowey-dowey cocktail she'd take a powder on, too. "You'll stress your heart," he kept saying to her; "there will be damage."

She had tried not to laugh in his face, *damage*! How clever and heart-stoppingly witless they were, these tenders of the body, how poised for perception that they'd never tumble to, and she had tried to check herself, tried to talk herself down off the jagged precipice of her anger. "He doesn't know," she'd say, "he didn't kill him—it was other doctors, this doctor is doing his best by you." But the rigid honesty of the precipice was better than the complicated emptiness of home, of trying to get on with one's life, of the pack of lies one told oneself in order to do so.

She listened to the stark, clear soprano voice singing, *Leçon de Ténèbres*, listened to the lamentations being sung, and envisioned the one candle in church on Maundy Thursdays being extinguished, and then another and another, until the snuffer came down on the fifteenth candle and there was just the cool, somber enormity of the stone church and the fine, fine, libidinal darkness. . . .

And she felt drawn to the darkness, drawn to how surprising and delicious darkness could be, coming from a movie onto the sidewalk, elation in her voice—"Oh, it's dark out"—or sitting for a time in the garden, drinking wine, her fork stirring every now and then, some bite brought to her mouth, and then the sudden realization, "Oh, it's gotten dark," and it could be so lovely, and seem so very precious, the palm trees perfectly blacked in across the sky.

She thought about her hand, invisible as it reached into his dark closet and moved his shirts along the rod, his shirts still fresh from the laundry in their clear plastic sheathes—that darkness—that darkness, too, was lovely, as was his smell in the dark closet, his smell still there after so many years, that darkness, his death, and the solace she still took in his clothes, or his signature in his books, the black ink in darkness, too, closed between book covers, or the many birthday cards he had written her that lived beneath her folded lingerie, sliding their infinitesimal distances each morning as she pulled open the dresser drawers. "Baby," they said, or "Sweetheart," or "My lover, my friend," all the sentiments kept in the sweet, cool darkness called intimacy, and, sure, sometimes she slid them from their tiny envelopes and lifted them into the dim light of their bedroom sconces, and the words were as alive to her as they had been opening them that first time, his happy face smiling at her—he loved giving her gifts. . . .

Their last moments had been in darkness, too, midnight, his body in hers, and the long precious ingot of darkness that stretched between their bodies as they lay against each other—that dark—that dark, too . . . but now her body was surrounded by light.

* * *

She set the phone down awkwardly on the tile counter and thought that was another reason to distrust plastic, its insipid little clatterings, and so then she did turn and move to the stove. She reached for the screeching kettle but then caught herself and took up a pot holder instead and lifted the kettle from the burner. She tapped her finger down against the small lever on the kettle's spout and the whistle stopped. She hadn't even warmed a mug yet, nor put coffee grounds in a filter; she hadn't touched that goddamn card with its insignia of twisted snakes, nor had she turned the flame off beneath the spider, and she watched the gas burn blue and coral and without purpose, without anything on top of it to boil. The flame might as well have been cold, but it wasn't, and she knew that if she set her hand down over it, her skin would crisp and burn, would become a kind of steak with too many bones. Could she eat it, she wondered, the thumb and four digits, a little sauce, some potatoes mashed with olive oil and garlic to mound up beneath the charred palm?

All the bright white things she was to trust and love, doctors doctoring during daylight hours, the hearty bleached fabric of their lab coats, their bright practiced smiles under the bright white fluorescent lights, and the bright white prescription pads, and all the bright white pages the drug studies had been printed on, and not one of these bright white knights had ever contacted her to ask her what she thought had happened to her husband. No, instead, one of the brightest in their field, a Los Angeles cardiologist, had derided her for having medical coverage from an HMO, this doctor she had paid $1675 to for a consultation on her husband's death—he had derided *her*, had said in one breath, "What quality of care did you expect from an HMO?" and "No, the care your husband received was just fine."

But the care her husband had received was not "just fine." In fact, he had really not had any care, just one prescription drug put on top of another and no doctor paying any attention. Nine months on a drug at its highest dosage, a drug to keep him well, a prophylactic, and no doctor bothered with a checkup, a monitor! Only a coroner in his windowless lab had been honest. "I see deaths from prescription drugs all of the time," he affirmed, "but usually anti-depressants."

She turned the knob on the stove slowly and the high flames guttered and shrank and disappeared and then fire took up again in the center ring, a small simmer of a flame and then no flame at all, just the black iron spider against the white enamel stove.

She walked across the kitchen to the cupboard and reached down one of their mugs—always a set they bought, two, their summer mugs, or the Christmas mugs, or the two beautiful majolica mugs garnered on a trip to San Francisco, all there in the cupboard like old couples, their handles arm in arm. She had tried to buy just one mug for herself, a special mug just for her and not one of a set, but that mug had leapt from her hands and shattered so joyously into the sink the second morning she'd had it . . .

. . . and she was not a dense woman, not impervious to omen or implication and my God, the sink seemed besotted with its blue shards! "Okay," she had said to this, too, "okay," because how else could she read this obvious archaeology, how else? The shards said, You will be alone now, but never alone again from the company of loss.

She listened to the Couperin, listened to Jeremiah's lament: "How lonely sits Jerusalem, that was full of people!

She has become like a widow." How singular this sounded being sung in Latin, the harpsicord beneath, and she thought that somehow the contemporary world forbade lamentation, forbade the rending of clothing and the gnashing of teeth, and it was something she had never allowed herself, either, any public display of grief, and yet one man had written on a blog that she had "sobbed" at the funeral in front of six hundred people, but he was writing out his own fictions; the most she had allowed herself was a word choked on here and there. What she had allowed to show was her anger, which, of course, was so much less acceptable. . . . Only God was allowed His anger, only God.

Now she ran the faucet until hot water came, and she placed a mug beneath the stream, one of a pair they'd bought in a small shop in Tahoe City, Italian, and painted with white flowers against a lattice of yellow and green bri-ars. Its mate sat on the shelf in the cupboard, sat there as though it looked down with propriety upon the coffee making. Okay, she thought, you get the card, and she picked the doctor's card up from its place before the coffee grinder, her thumb atop the twisted snakes, and pulled open the glass-fronted cupboard and dropped it into the mug. Stay there for a while, she murmured, and then she took down a brown paper filter and a filter cone.

In the grinder, there was ground coffee already, and a powder snowed darkly down upon her hand as she lifted the lid and emptied the coffee, as dark as glacial soil, into the filter. Sometimes ground coffee smelled like tuna, one of the odd truths of the world, but this morning it smelled like the rich Italian roast that it was. Why go, she thought, why go to a doctor at all? She knew a woman named

Catherine who hadn't been to one for almost fifty years, and Catherine's own father had been a doctor, but there was a bit of the "mortification of the flesh" about Catherine, too. And unlike Catherine, she wasn't exactly ready to hang herself upside down like a flower to dry, her head full of blood, her body friable. Desiccation would come whether she exalted it or not.

She emptied the hot water from the mug and then fitted the filter to its lip and passed across the kitchen to the stove. How beautiful the hot water made the coffee grounds as she bloomed them, first a small amount of water, just to moisten, just to plump, and then she swamped the cone with water and stood, waiting, the kettle held aloft, and then she swamped the filter again.

How much damage to the heart? she wondered, and then she knew what for, the doctor, knew why she'd make an appointment and go. *Information.* She was going to the doctor for information, and then she laughed, thinking that was precisely what Eve had been up against with that serpent, too: "You surely shall not die." Hadn't that been what that snake had promised, also?

Thorns

⬧⬦⬧

In college the young woman thinks she should be able to read faster, to see after a few hours' quiet an appreciable advance in the placement of the bookmark. It seems her classmates have terrific speed, and because of this speed, terrific confidence: How else can they proceed to read so intrepidly? Biochemistry, statistics, these are slow going for everyone, but Henry James, Shakespearean plays, her classmates read these in just a few hours' time, minutes really, and then they are off to Copper Mountain, a movie. How do they understand it so quickly and with so little anguish? One hundred and fifty dollars for ten weeks' instruction every Wednesday evening at seven: The Art of Speed Reading.

The instructor notices her immediately, the young woman at the back of the class, and close to the window, which she looks out of often, too often, so that he wonders fiercely if he bores her. Of course, they've barely gotten started and he is covering merely the preliminaries, the disclaimers, the hype, the rates of speed that can be acquired, *Middlemarch* in three hours. . . . He'll ask her for coffee, take her to Pearl Street, find out what draws her interest beyond his classroom.

"The garden," she says simply at the café, and then adds, because he seems not quite to understand, "the forsythia in bloom."

"So, you into flowers?" he asks, leaning forward in his chair, tucking his hands into his arms, eager.

"I suppose you could say I'm *into* flowers, yes."

"Something wrong with the way I said that?" he asks seriously.

"No," she says, and he hears the note of resignation in her voice. "What are you into?" she asks him, "I mean besides being *into* speed-reading classes?"

"So you're sensitive to words. You don't like that phrasing, 'into something'?"

"It seems about right for skateboards. How did you become interested in teaching?"

"Specifically teaching, or teaching speed reading?" he asks. "I'd like a keoke coffee," he says to the waitress, and then, turning briskly to the young woman, inquires, "What do you want? You want to share a piece of cake or something?"

The young woman doesn't much care which question he answers about teaching or speed reading, but she wonders why simple powers of observation don't instruct him in how to take someone for coffee, in how to order. "I haven't even looked at the menu yet," she says to the waitress. "Could you just give me a moment?"

"Sure," the waitress says, "I'll just order this and come right back."

"No," the young woman says evenly. "Why don't you wait to order his so that we might drink something together—that would be the point, wouldn't it, to drink something together?"

"Oh, okay, sure," the waitress whispers sweetly, and then adds, "Some people want theirs really fast."

The young woman feels instantly chagrined, because, of course, the waitress is right, some people do want theirs very fast, and this guy, Kevin, is surely one of those people. "What do *you* like to drink?" she asks quickly, but the waitress is already scooting away down their row of tables. People mass three-deep at the bar, and at the counter, where the waiters and waitresses shout orders, a policeman stands with a Chihuahua tucked beneath his arm. He bobs his shoulders right and then left, a great show of allowing the wait-people access to the counter. He seems to know quite distinctly that he impedes business standing where he stands, and yet he remains steadfast, his eyes on the man at the cappuccino machine, the dog's tail twitching against the dark blue of his uniform.

"Want to divide something?" the speed-reading instructor asks again. "I really like the carrot cake. Plus, it's not quite so unhealthy for you as the others."

The young woman turns back to the table and smiles at him. "Would that be because of the half cup of grated carrots?" she comments, meaning to tease him.

"Yeah," he agrees, encouraged by her smile. "I guess you're right. But it's good carrot cake."

"Why, then, don't you order a piece—a piece for yourself," she specifies.

He nods and then reaches up and loosens his tie, yanking right and then left. "So, okay, what's this flower called?" he asks, pointing at the green Perrier bottle on the table. "You know flowers so well."

She doesn't bother to counter him, to say that she has never claimed to know flowers "so well." "They're called alstroemeria," she says, "and sometimes, in the vernacular, Peruvian lilies."

"How'd you get interested in flowers?" he asks easily, glancing off into the restaurant and then back at her.

"I suppose I find it puzzling that anyone isn't just innately interested in flowers," she says. "They're beautiful."

"So, you like beauty?"

He exhausts her, his inability to distinguish what is talked about and what remains observed, noted. He's just a guy trying to be nice to me, she reminds herself, a sweet-enough guy, whose attentions will flatter someone else immensely.

"I'm sorry," she says. "I shouldn't have come out. I've been very tired recently."

"Seems like maybe you're tired a lot?" he proposes. His voice sounds hopeful, and not unkind.

"You haven't told me yet how you got interested in teaching," she says, "or in speed reading, for that matter?"

"I just always hated to read as a kid, hated how long it took me, and then you'd get tested on just a few things and it seemed sort of useless, all that writing, which you had to read but which wasn't important." And then the waitress stands at their table, wanting their order.

"Do you have something called a blondie?" the young woman asks her. "It's sort of a butterscotch brownie."

"Sure do," the waitress says, and later, when the speed-reading instructor and the young woman are in the parking structure, standing just inside the elevator, the young woman can still hear the waitress's cheery voice, her equilibrium, can still see what appears like an abiding kindness in the waitress's eyes.

"I've really forgotten what floor I parked on," the speed-reading instructor says, concerned. He ponders the bank of buttons, his hand hovering. "God, I have no idea." He turns to look at her, and she sees that he's uncomfortable, anxious, maybe even a little ashamed.

"I think we're on the bottom floor," she offers. "Because at the elevator doors, there was only one button to push, right? There was only an up button?"

He pushes P-4, the lowest level of parking, and then turns back to her. "I hate that type of intelligence," he says, smiling, sheepish. "I mean—you know what I mean, I don't hate it at all."

But of course she does know what he means, has learned in this very moment why she equally attracts and repels him. "Sure," she says as cheerily as she can muster. "I know what you mean." But she feels no equilibrium, no abiding kindness, only a great desperation to be at home, alone among pictures of the species roses of Sichuan and Yunnan in western China. Blossoming first yellow, the yellow deepening into pink, a purplish pink, then crimsoning, these single five-petaled roses bloom from solitary shrubs along stream banks or along paths between rice fields, and sometimes, sometimes, in the sunlight of July and August, their huge crimson thorns glisten like molten glass. The thorns glisten, she thinks as the elevator falls slowly, the thorns glisten like vitriol.

She smiles at him, a mastered smile, and she says, "Did you know that the French encase their nuclear waste in glass—they vitrify it?" and she reflects a face she has just now made for him, polishes up her eyes into a welcome, feels her cheeks lift into shiny reception. She sees the sparkle of her jewelry and the silver threads purling through her sweater; she sees the ground fish scales within her face powder—a glitter—and the lovely manners she can wipe clean with a lintless towel, she can make crystaline. She will encase what is caustic deeply beyond a glassy surface.

This friendly decent bumblebee of a man infuriates her, and though he has gone in search of sweetness, he will bump absently against what will now be her obsidian kindness.

He looks at her with a very long, steady gaze. The elevator bottoms squeakily and he asks, as though forced to ask, "What made you think of that? Just now."

The elevator doors break open. "It's something my father once told me. I don't know why I thought of it. But it was always very compelling to me—the vitreous solidity holding tight the caustic, the volatile. I wondered if all around the coast of France the deep sea wasn't aglow with massive radioactive glass spheres? I wondered if they were beautiful or not, like Dale Chihuly flowers," she says, looking up at him, excited. She is very excited. "Perhaps they're like hydras or anemones, like huge glass polyps!" but seeing his seriousness, she feels foolish. Maybe they're like medusas, she thinks, like her own reflection glistening beneath the onyx water.

She thinks to tell him something hard, factual, something not passionate so he will not be so afraid of her, some detail she will speak in a clear, simple voice leached of emotion, a tone to assure him that she is sweetness and light. "Did you know," she says, "did you know that thorns are modified branches?"

But he continues to stare at her, and she thinks, *Tiny woody spines encased in gathers of molten glass though we want to think of this as sunshine.*

Gut

···❖···

I met Herb standing in a knife store in a little town in Massachusetts. Newly arrived to the coast, I was trying to get with the program, and I wanted an oyster knife. I thought I'd throw a little party, oysters on the half shell and a few bottles of good crisp Sancerre, nothing too dear, but good Sancerre nonetheless. I loved oysters, but I'd never opened one in my life. I'd worked my way through art school waiting tables in a pretty decent little French bistro in Chicago and so I knew something about food, but now that I wasn't eating at the family table every night before the dinner service, it took some effort to eat the way I'd so happily eaten for four years.

"I'm very excited," I said to this man standing behind me, waiting for the shopkeep just like I was. "I've never owned an oyster knife."

"Is that what you think that is?" he asked. He seemed very serious, as though perhaps I'd discovered a rare species of oyster knife, one never seen in these northern parts.

"Yes," I said. "Do you think it's hard to learn how to shuck an oyster?"

"Well, with a clam knife it might be," he said.

I laughed, thinking that was kind of funny, an it's-not-hard-unless-you-make-it-hard kind of response. I turned back to the counter, but the man in front of me, paying, seemed bothered by something. Even though it was summer, he wore a canvas barn coat.

"You're telling me," he kept saying, and the shopkeep would respond, "I am." This exchange happened three or four times, but what it was about, I had no idea. "Goddamn it to hell," he said, reaching into his huge coat pocket, "you're telling me?"

"I am."

"Excuse me," I heard the man behind me murmur. I twisted around, happy to talk to someone, to anyone really. I'd been fairly lonely since arriving in town, and the party was to help me out of the doldrums a bit. I thought the best way for me to meet people was to invite them over and make them meet me. Two months ago, I'd responded to a query in the *New York Times* classifieds: "Washington-style handpress, C. Foster & Brother, Cincinnati, 1852. Needs care and use."

"Excuse me," he said again. "Do you know what noise annoys an oyster?"

He had a deep voice and the words seemed to get pronounced very carefully. He was maybe thirty-five years old. I didn't know, and I wasn't good with men's ages anyway, as it seemed like not much of an accurate measure. I laughed again. "What noise annoys an oyster," I repeated. It was fun to say.

"A noisy noise annoys an oyster," he said seriously, and then the bell on the door jangled and I turned and saw the barn jacket departing and realized it was my turn to step up and pay.

"Hey, Herb," the shopkeep said, looking past me, lifting his huge paw of a hand. His gaze came back to me and he smiled. "This all you want?" he asked.

"Yes," I said, "just the oyster knife."

"Why you bringing me a clam knife, then?" he asked.

"Oh." I stumbled about. "It was in a bin with a sign. It said 'oyster knives—fifteen ninety-five?'"

"Well, fine, but that won't make this an oyster knife. Herb, you want to show this sweet wee thing what an oyster knife looks like. My knee is bad again today."

"I'm sorry to hear that," Herb said. "Why don't you get a stool for back there behind the counter?"

"I've got a stool," he responded disgustedly, shaking his big head.

"Do you have those cushioned pads back there for the floor, you know, the ones they use in restaurants? Those might help, too."

"Sure. They might."

And I was standing there while these two locals exchanged niceties that seemed like they might extend into tomorrow night. Finally, Herb said, "Just a minute," and he sidled down a narrow aisle of cutting boards and then came springing back, playing with the knife as if it were a ninja sword, though it was only about five inches long. He placed it on the old wooden counter as though I were a wild animal he was trying to tame and the knife being laid down was to reassure me, to calm me.

It didn't look right. The blade was narrower and it curved in and then out again. "That's an oyster knife? Really?" I queried. I knew graving instruments, but here I was out of my field.

"Now, Herb." The shopkeep was shaking his head. "Come on, now."

"So, what's this knife for?" I asked, because now I was in on the game.

Herb moved the clam knife a few inches on the counter. "That," he said, "is a clam knife, and that," he went on, lining up the latest knife on the counter, "is a scallop knife, and this—" he paused, pulling something from his back pocket—"is an oyster knife." It was thick handled and the knife part was barely a nubbin, not a blade at all. "When are you planning to shuck these oysters?" Herb asked. "Maybe I could help."

"That would be good," I said. "I accept. Tomorrow evening around seven. I live—"

"I know all about where you live," Herb said quickly. He had pulled out his wallet and was laying a twenty-dollar bill down across the oyster knife, as though he was paying for it.

"You know where I live?" I asked, watching this. "I mean, *why* do you know where I live?" I picked up Herb's money and pushed it down his front shirt pocket. He smelled good, sandalwood and spice, but then something not quite human.

"It's my parents' property you're renting," he said, pulling the bill out. "John, don't take this sweet wee one's money—'sweet wee one'—you got some way with language!"

John guffawed. "I think I said 'sweet wee thing,' but who's arguing?"

"Don't sell her an oyster knife until after tomorrow. I'll get her trained up, and that way we'll avoid a trip to the emergency room."

"Sure thing."

"Which brings me to why I'm here. Mom wants to know if you can cater the rehearsal dinner for Betsy's wedding. It's August twelfth. Twenty, at most twenty-five, and she wants lobster, clams, mussels, and down from the house, if you don't mind."

"I've used your mother's outdoor kitchen a few times before, but there's no seaweed in that stretch—"

"Yeah, well, I eat it all," Herb said, and they both laughed.

The shopkeep pulled out a small ledger from beneath the counter. "I'll bring some up from Mitre Point."

I suppose my face had a look on it that imparted that here was something else I was left out of, because Herb held out his hand. "Herb Wallace," he said to me, "and this is John Sumell."

"Pleased to meet you," I said, though this seemed not quite all I needed by way of introduction. We were well past names, even if I didn't know them till this moment.

"Herb's up at Harvard," John Sumell said, though how that explained eating seaweed, I wasn't sure. I have never been fond of shaking hands with men, with anyone really. Nonetheless, I held my hand out at the suggestion of advanced education.

"Where are Betsy's new folks from?" John Sumell asked as he threw open the ledger and penned in "12 August/Wallace/25."

"John," Herb began, looking down at me squint-eyed, "we're breaking in a lot of new people this summer— 'sweet wee thing' here, and Betsy's guy is from North Carolina, and I assume his folks are, too. They all seemed very excited about a clambake, and since they're paying for it, have at it."

John Sumell nodded his big head as if to say he'd fleece the Southerners as best he knew how but that fleecing people wasn't really his thing.

"I really want an oyster knife," I pleaded, because I could see that they both thought they were done with me. I had taken my wallet out and was pulling bills from its inner folds. "Look," I said, "I promise I won't try to use this until you're there tomorrow, but at least let me buy one."

Herb pointed to the wall behind the old cash register.

"What?" I said.

On the wall was the requisite detritus of old shops, two-dollar bills and a calendar featuring songbirds, except on this wall there was also an array of invitations to celebrations and parties and weddings, and the invitations were mostly beautiful and elegant, on cotton or linen stock, and engraved. I knew what I was looking at because I'm a printmaker, and this was no batch of invites downloaded from the computer. I was looking at thousands of dollars spent at Tiffany or Dempsey & Carroll. I could also see a couple of hand-set letterpress creations with hand-torn edges. Jesus, I thought, old money.

"I'm sorry," I said, because I still couldn't figure out what was being pointed out. There was a large oval of wood with one long word carved into it, but the word looked Algonquin, or some Indian language now spoken by three hundred people. Herb Wallace pointed directly at this.

KWITCHURBELYAKIN

John Sumell turned and sat down heavily on his stool. "Well, sound it out," he said.

Herb was looking at me seriously, not saying anything.

"Oh, okay," I then said, sort of amused and sort of not so amused. I really wanted an oyster knife.

"What are you making for those oysters tomorrow night?" John Sumell asked.

"A *mignonette*," I said. "Just a light one, vinegar, shallots—"

"What kind of vinegar?" he asked.

"Tarragon?" I proposed tentatively.

"Good girl," he said, and that was it. I was excused. Herb was holding the door for me. "See you tomorrow at seven," he said.

Well, I was pissed, but then I teased myself out of it by saying, "You wanted to meet people!"

Herb and I had one of those rehearsal-dinner lobster clambakes, and our wedding invitation hangs on John's wall today, still, and my baby brother and a slew of Herb's male friends shucked oysters behind a long table at our wedding reception. We didn't feed each other cake; we fed each other a raw oyster on the half shell—it was very sexy and I can still feel that delicious salty oyster seawater trickling down my throat. I don't know how to shuck an oyster—or rather, I do know the mechanics, but I've never to this day done it myself. Of course, the women looked beautiful at our wedding, the silk dresses fluttering in the ocean breezes, but my favorite picture will always be that line of beautiful young men in white shirts and ties, standing behind the long table, each holding a folded towel in one hand and an oyster knife in the other. They'd shuck one oyster for a guest and then pop the next one in their own mouths, and of course they'd been throwing back the beers. The heap of half shells by dinnertime was huge, and there's another picture of a champagne bottle pushed into the pile and one of the caterers in a long white apron walking away, the ocean in the distance. God, we had fun.

For the honeymoon, Herb said he'd long been interested in the Yahgan hunter-gatherers of Tierra del Fuego and that maybe I'd like to see the southern-most tip of South America. "Ess-Dubya-Tee," he said, playing on the initials for "sweet wee thing," "the Yahgan use sea lion gut to make a sausage of blubber and various soft-tissue organs. Maybe that'd just be really delicious." Herb added this last casually. I said we'd be hunting and gathering on the Faubourg Saint-Honoré and that if I was going anywhere with the word *south* in it, it was the south of France. I suggested we rent a car and drive from Paris to Orléans and down the Loire to Sancerre. After all, I knew what to do with a bottle of Sancerre. I sang "I Got You, Babe" to Herb as we walked through customs at Charles de Gaulle, but for our third anniversary, he managed to get me to a remote highland station in Papua New Guinea, where he studied Mae Enga patri-clans and whether or not they shared their food, and I sheltered within a leaky hut perched on a forested ridge in the pouring rain and all the drawing paper I'd brought curled into a mildewed heap by day two. Mae Enga men don't reside with their womenfolk, but family pigs do, and consequently, upon our return stateside, it took American doctors six months to rid my body of ringworm.

I am grateful that my baby brother got himself married and his bride pregnant and produced a son who adores his famous biological anthropologist uncle, because without Jamie, I'd have to accompany Herb on one excursion after another, and last summer's was Alaska, where the diet of the Inuit was up for inspection and frozen reindeer turds a must-eat delicacy. "Darling," I said to my nephew upon their return, "I'm leaving you everything!" Unfortunately, "leaving you everything" means very little to someone who is eleven years old and willing to eat shit.

For several years now, Herb's primary inquiry has been how the human digestive system shrank and the human brain subsequently grew—at least he thinks that's the sequence of evolutionary events: once our colon got downsized, our brain could upsize. Man cooking his food supposedly brought this about. Once we started building fires and roasting up the kill, the calories were much more readily available and so our gut didn't have to work so hard and that energy could go into creating our tremendous brains. I've lived with Herb developing this research for years now, and he's never bored me a minute, but my ability to be a loving helpmate was being taxed this summer. Jamie had gotten football and now there was a camp my brother and sister-in-law were sending him to to ruin his well-made bones, and suddenly he wasn't available for excursions with his uncle. I used to worry that my nephew might be in some dangerous situation with Herb, or that Herb would have him eat some plant that might prove fatal to Jamie. Now that two-hundred-pound teenagers were hurling themselves at my nephew and my brother seemed willing to pay for this mosh pit called sport, I actively campaigned to have Jamie free for his uncle's uses. So what if he had to have his stomach pumped; he wasn't going to sustain a head injury sorting seeds out of orangutan feces.

Part of Herb's research has to do with trying to locate just when in the evolutionary process humans went from eating raw food, like our relatives the chimps, to cooking it. This summer, Herb thought it might provide further evidence to eat the food that chimpanzees eat, to see if we like it better than, say, the food that other kinds of primates eat, ones supposedly we didn't evolve from. He theorizes that we'll accommodate chimpanzee grub better than that of gorillas or bonobos or what have you, even if our jaws and dentition are now different.

At first when Herb said to me one morning in early June, "Ess-Dubya-Tee, we're going on a diet this summer," I said to myself, Yes, I suppose it's about time, although I hadn't thought I'd been putting on the pounds. I do a lot of standing—carving woodcuts and rolling prints isn't the most sedentary of the arts—but I'd rounded out a bit for sure. There hadn't been any "There's more to hold on to here than I need" comments, but still my first thought as a woman, and as one very much in love with her husband, was, I'm sorry. Of course I'll go on a diet!

"You're about finished with the cuts for that book, right?" he asked, moving the blue porcelain salt and pepper shakers together on the table. He'd been using them for his boiled egg, and now he straightened the table as though he were out-maneuvering the Japanese on a map of the Pacific theater. What on earth? I thought to myself. My guy is not exactly an attentive domestic, though he is keenly interested in how domesticity came about. "Wanna go to Africa for a month?" he asked, eyeing me like I might say yes if he was really really careful with where the butter dish ended up in his intricate re-arrangement of the breakfast table.

"Sweetheart," I said, "what are you doing?"

"What?" he said, with the requisite amount of hurt male pride. "What?"

"Since when do you straighten the dishes on the breakfast table?"

"That's a deeper question than you might imagine," he said, and we both laughed. We always laughed together, but that had gotten me into more situations with Herb than I can recount.

"Let's start at the beginning," I said, sighing, but I was amused. He was wearing a pale blue shirt and he has pale blue eyes and the porcelain on the table is pale blue and it all seemed staged and dramatic and compelling.

"Well, we pretty much know a lot about the beginning," he said. "It's the middle years that we're interested in here."

"And so the diet is what?" I knew to ask.

"Would you like to go to Africa? Just answer that question."

"Just answer 'Would you like to go to Africa?'"

"Yes, would you like to go to Africa? We'd be in Kibale, at the Chimpanzee Project."

"And eat what?" I quickly asked. Suddenly, Herb seemed fantastically interested in the jam pot. "Herb?"

"I think what would concern you most is not so much *what*, but for how long."

"Good," I said, coaxing him, "that's a start—"

"Four or five hours a day," he said, moving the lid of the jam pot around so that its spoon came out at a rakish angle.

"We're talking about eating?" I asked, puzzled. "We'd be eating four or five hours a day?"

He looked sheepish, and then he straightened up in his chair. "For starters," he pronounced, taking on a professorial voice, but I was no graduate student being trained in contingency; I knew my darling biological anthropologist husband down to his long beautiful feet—and he did have beautiful feet.

"So, sweetheart, what you're breaking to me gently is that you'd like to take me to Africa and fatten me up for what—five hours a day, probably more like seven hours a day? Is that accurate?"

"I suppose it could be eight hours, but I think seven hours is about right. We'd have to see how much it took to maintain your weight."

"Which nicely gets us to the question of *what* I'd be eating," I said, but I was already reaching for the telephone sitting in its cubby surrounded by cookbooks. I had most of my brother's telephone number dialed before Herb answered my question.

"Greens," he said simply. "Leaves."

"And my reward for losing weight would be that I had to eat more leaves?" I asked incredulously, but then it dawned on me that the answer was "of course!" "And what else?" I quickly asked. "What other charming comestibles?" I finished dialing my brother, and when Jamie answered, I said, "Jamie, this is your aunt, and if you love me, you'll give up this absurd idea of playing football and go with your uncle to Africa."

"You want to talk to Dad?" he asked without missing a beat.

"How old are you?" I said.

"I don't know," he said, "twelve, I guess."

"What do you mean, you guess? Make a decision, for God's sake. Africa—sound good to you? All expenses paid."

"I have practice," he said, "but here's Dad," and my nephew was gone from the line.

"Abby?" my brother queried.

"Hold on a minute," I said, covering the mouthpiece with my hand. "What else are we talking about here, Herb?"

"Raw meat, and the chimps seem to mix leaves with the meat, and something about that seems to shorten the time they have to spend eating every day—see, some good news there," he offered, smiling at me with his eyes. He was folding his napkin in quarters and tucking it down alongside his plate. He straightened his spoon and knife beside the eggcup. "It would just be a month," he said, reaching for the cream pitcher and moving it beside the sugar bowl.

"Matt—it's Abby, and Herb would like to take Jamie to the preserve in Africa for a month. This is the opportunity of a lifetime. What other twelve-year-old kid gets to spend a month in Africa with his uncle?"

"We've already talked about it," my brother said. His voice sounded strained.

"Who's 'we'?"

"Herb and I have talked about it already and Jamie can't go and we all think you'd have a very good time and that you could do some woodcuts of the animals."

Now I was in a fix, because I couldn't counter by saying I wouldn't have any time to do woodcuts, because if I revealed that either Jamie or I would be spending upward of eight hours a day chewing our food, I'd never manage to get Jamie's parents to agree to his going. "I can do woodcuts from photographs," I said, "and anyway, what an opportunity for Jamie, don't you agree?"

"Football," my brother said definitively, a tone of voice he was good at because he's a philosophy professor.

"We have evolved this far only to train our children to hurl themselves at one another?" I asked, meaning every word of my question.

"And Jamie doesn't really like that much roughage," Matt went on, laughing now.

"Herb told you what he'd be eating? Really?" I asked, somewhat impressed.

"Of course I did," Herb interjected. "What do you think, I'd take my nephew halfway around the world and not tell his parents what I was going to do with him?"

"Are you telling me that Jamie will eat frozen reindeer turds but he won't eat leaves?"

Herb got up and left the breakfast room and then Roy Buchanan's guitar playing sounded from his den with all its intricate roving sexiness. Oh man, he really wants me to go to Africa, I thought to myself. I had a hard time turning Herb down when he put Buchanan on. We always ended up making love.

"Matt," I began, "come on, let Jamie go."

"He's getting made fun of at school, Abby."

"Why on earth?" I asked seriously. I stood up to clear the table while I was talking and then the phone went dead. I held the handset away from me, that stupid thing we all do, as though looking at the handset will make someone's voice suddenly come back on the line. I put the phone down and then picked up our breakfast plates and took them to the sink in the kitchen. Where were those lovely, willing graduate students when you needed them? Though I didn't exactly think this was a very wise bit of experiential research to inflict on young people, no matter how willing they were. Jamie seemed the perfect foil for Herb. A relative, one he loved, and so one whose health he wasn't inclined to take chances with. Plus, Herb knew I'd never speak to him again if he harmed my nephew. I wasn't convinced Herb was ever sufficiently careful with a graduate student, but then again, graduate students were so damn intelligent, I couldn't trust them not to come up with even wilder ideas than my husband.

Finally the phone rang. "Why is Jamie being made fun of in school?" I asked by way of answering.

"Abby, I'm with you on this one," my sister-in-law, Carrie, said. "I'd love for Jamie to go to Africa instead of going to football camp. Africa would be cheaper than this frigging camp, too."

Strangely, I wondered just when my sister-in-law hadn't been "with" me on something, but I let it go. "What's happening at school?" I asked again.

"Well, you know, he's surrounded by artists and egg-heads at home—"

"Matt thinks he should be raised so that he fits in on a playground or a football field?" I asked, interrupting her. "That's a pretty low bar," I said, fiercely disappointed in what I was hearing.

"It's Jamie, Abby. *He* wants to fit in."

Carrie's voice sounded pained and resolved. I could see her leaned against her desk in her office, twirling the red cord on her telephone. She ran a small business brokering cran-berries, believe it or not, and she'd cornered the bog market. She wasn't a dunce and I didn't want to push her, and Buchanan's guitar was screaming in the background. "Okay," I finally said into the telephone, and not very happily.

"You're probably not going to die," she said, trying to be lighter. "You'll devolve, and your brow will lower, but hey, you'll be really thin."

"I've heard better wit in my life," I said, thinking, she's not an artist or an egghead. Disgruntlement didn't quite describe my state of mind. "How's the Thanksgiving rush?"

"Cranberries aren't really just seasonal anymore—"

"I know. It's called making conversation," I said quickly, because now I was really annoyed. I could not see how football practice or camp or Jamie's pursuing a ball up and down a patch of grass could trump a trip to Africa with his uncle, and it wasn't about the research, either, about chowing down on foliage for a month; it was about experience and opportunity and education. I was astounded, too, as though my brother's family had chosen to have a McDonald's Big Mac instead of lobster, though maybe food analogies—*homo sapiens* food analogies—weren't quite in order here.

Not only did Herb and I go to Africa and eat chimpanzee feed for a month, but there were periods of diet change in which the shoots and bark orangutans eat and the ones gorillas eat were put before me for comparison. Herb had a easier time getting it all down, and keeping it down, but I threw up a grand total of thirty-six times, and then some enzyme or microbe kicked in and my colon seemed better able to accommodate the various chunks of raw meat mixed with leaves. Let me put it this way: Constipation was not a problem, but pooping while you ate was just not the type of multi-tasking I was up to. I did start steering clear of meat, however, because it took twice as long to chew and I'd lost a lot of weight by that time. Herb said I was acting exactly like a chimpanzee, that chimps love meat but that they get tired of chewing it, too. This seemed to excite him no end, that both the chimps and I would give meat a rest. My jaw hurt so much, I didn't even bother trying to question him. Certainly speech came about after human guts shrank and we didn't have to spend seven hours a day chewing leaves. I found it just painful to make my mouth form words and then to push them out into the heavy, moist air of Uganda.

I have to admit, bamboo shoots are tastier than one might think, and it dawned on me within a few days just how many leaves humans eat—lettuce and grape leaves and shiso and herbs, and collards and chard and mustard, and we eat hearts of palm and leeks, which are shoots, and onions and plenty of roots, too, and tubers. Nuts and seeds. We'd gotten fancy about presentation, perhaps, but a collard is a collard is a collard. And sure, of course, cooking—we'd begun to cook most of these leaves—but I started to formulate some different theories about why our guts had shrunk. Herb seemed pretty inclined toward the alimentary, that food tasted better and was more easily digestible and didn't need such a huge gut, and that cooked chow gave us a readier energy source, but I secretly wondered if our desire for speech hadn't piggy-backed handily on the baser evolutionary journey, nudged it along perhaps, the freedom of our mouths to make speech as vital and imperative a desire as the one to survive. Something had to make all that fighting and running and terror worthwhile. I also wondered if singing weren't the relaxation of screaming?

Herb began to be overly attentive sexually, and I said to him one early morning before the chewing had begun, "All of your research is bogus."

"What?" he asked, distractedly. There was a huge pile of young bamboo shoots beside the table, and in the mottled morning light it looked remarkably like the skirt of a ballgown by Valentino.

"Bogus," I said loudly across the tent. I was so damn sick—and sick of all of this. I thought it was going to be a purely fruit day, and usually that was better, figs and plantains and pawpaws, but the acids in my stomach were at gale force. Herb found this profoundly interesting, too. Aside from humans, all other primates prefer fruit and will go to great lengths to eat it if it's available. The fact that my stomach was not happy with so much fruit seemed the ultimate to Herb in interesting details.

"Why 'bogus'?" he asked, finally turning from his logs to look at me. He sat on an upturned wooden box at a rickety campaign table, but then he got up and came to the cot where I'd been sleeping. He sidled in alongside me, shedding his shorts as he did. "Why?" he said, nuzzling me with his nose and chin, and with that other long protuberance of his. He reached his long arm down beneath his own cot and pushed the play button on his boom box. Roy Buchanan's blues guitar came on and "Green Onions" held its own against the cacaphony of a Ugandan morning.

"Because you like me thin like this," I said, "and you're more sexually aroused than I've ever seen you, and so of course I'm going to eat what has brought that about, whether or not I like its taste. Your research posits that the females are making feed decisions based on taste and health and physical need. When on earth do you think a female ate what she wanted to eat around a male?"

"That's interesting," Herb said. "Maybe a rather good theory about sexual dimorphism."

"What?" I said, trying to push away from him a bit so that I could see his face. "I thought muscle mass had to do with sex hormones."

"Did you know that gorillas are having face-to-face sex now?" He said this with great relish, looking down at me, opening my legs with his knee—he just loved this stuff.

"When they're performing cunnilingus, then I want to hear about it," I said, relaxing, pushed as deeply into the cot as I could be. "And what about kissing?" I asked. "Why wouldn't the desire to do something with our mouths other than eat drive evolution?"

"Stopping on the savanna to give blow jobs is probably not going to help survival rates," Herb said offhandedly, and I thought to myself, Wow. I think of speech and song and kissing and Herb goes straight to blow job. Could one species be evolving along two different evolutionary paths at the same time? But Herb was a beautiful lover. and that morning was no different. His breath across my face felt like silk, and oddly, somewhere deep at the base of my throat, I could feel how deeply he was inside me, but then he reached under my cot and brought up a long stick covered in small pale beige flies with transparent wings. "These are termites," he said, "and chimps use sticks to fish for them. We thought we'd see if you liked them."

Herb lay alongside me on the cot and I looked into his blue eyes and they seemed as kind and loving and serious as ever. The acid came into my throat and I started to cry, deep throbs coming up out of my chest—the thought of divorce was so painful. Herb reached across under his cot and turned off Buchanan's guitar work. I heard a sudden racket of chimpanzees screeching and then Mbele stood just inside the tent flap, holding a bamboo tray. He was smiling mirthfully and he knelt down so that I could see, but at first I didn't even recognize the china because there were preciously thin slices of toast standing up on end, glistening with butter, and pale yellow scrambled eggs crossed with smoked salmon and heaped with caviar. Then, because I smelled coffee, I saw the perfectly lovely little pot banded with green leaves and acorns, and the tiny sugar bowl and cream pitcher. How many years ago had I seen this porcelain breakfast set in Paris at Bernardaud? And even then it had cost over two thousand dollars.

Herb—naked as a gorilla—rolled off my cot and dragged over the wooden box he used for a stool. He had Mbele set the tray down. I struggled up, pulling the rough camp sheet around me. The coffee, the eggs, the toast—it all smelled unbelievably delicious. I was perhaps less embarrassed than I should have been that Mbele had obviously been at the tent flap for some time, listening for whatever the cue was that he and Herb had agreed upon. They were in such cahoots. Tears still coursed down my face and I was suddenly terrified that Herb really did want me to eat the termites and that then— only then—would I be able to have my eggs with salmon and caviar, but Herb held a fork in one hand, and on it was a small mound of eggs, and beneath this he held a piece of glistening toast. Mbele moved quietly about the tent, setting up his instruments, and Herb moved the fork to my mouth and the food melted across my tongue, soft and warm and delicious. Being fed that first taste of buttery eggs and smoked salmon and caviar after the month of leaves—only the oyster in its trickle of seawater had ever tasted as delicious—and he fed me the entire plate and then because I must have still looked ravenous for human fare, he pursed his lips and shook his head.

"I just don't think it's a good idea. See how that sits on your stomach, and if it does, Cook'll make you up another plate."

"It's over?" I asked. "We're done? No more bamboo?"

I heard a deep laugh emanate from Mbele as he rolled up the canvas tent flap and tied it back, his fine long fingers moving like great spiders. Sunlight infused the tent and then I saw an outline of Mbele's dark body like a silhouette surrounded by ecru paper. Mbele turned and looked back into the tent, but I couldn't see his features.

"Stop making fun of the white folk, Mbele," I said, and he moved a little into the tent so that I could see his face.

"What would compel me to stop?" he asked with a London accent, and we both laughed. He came over on the other side of the cot and hunkered down. He lifted my wrist and, looking down, counted my pulse. "I have a gift for you," he then said. "May I bring it to you?"

"No more jokes this morning," I said. "No ants, no termites, no—"

"No, of course not. No more jokes, Dr. Wallace," Mbele said.

"No more jokes, Dr. Ruwenzori," Herb said seriously.

Mbele gently laid my wrist back down atop the sheet and then stuck a thermometer in my mouth. "We're frightening the females," he said.

"Do you know she married me for a printing press?" Herb was pulling on a pair of khaki shorts and I watched as he pushed the buttons through their holes and then buckled the cloth belt.

"It used to be so much easier, a hunk of raw meat—"

"—chasing off the fraternity—" And then there was Jamie standing in the bright light of the tent opening, his arm in a huge plaster cast.

"Hi, Aunt Abby," he said sheepishly.

"You are so effing late," I said.

"Yeah, but I brought the caviar and the smoked salmon."

"Did you, darling?" I said, smiling around the length of glass in my mouth.

"Yes, okay, so he did, but I'd like credit for the china," Herb said, "and for the printing press, too, while I'm at it."

"Oh, Jesus," I said, laughing, but then it was all so quickly in my throat and mouth and Mbele grabbed the thermometer before it hit the bowl he held miraculously beneath my face. "That's thirty-seven," he said, and Herb walked over to his table and entered something in his log.

"What's thirty-seven?" Jamie asked, and then it suddenly seemed to dawn on him. "You mean Aunt Abby's barfed thirty seven times? Really? Wow!"

I wiped my face with the cloth that Mbele handed me. "I hope to hell you brought more than smoked salmon and caviar—not that I'm complaining."

"Dad," Jamie ventured.

"No, not your father," I snapped.

"Oh, good, 'cause he's still in Entebbe." And the way the Bantu name—pronounced correctly—came so easily from Jamie's mouth made me happy.

"What's the name of the airport in Amsterdam?" I asked him. "You came through Amsterdam, right?"

"Schiphol," he answered tentatively.

"Yes," I said, and then I pointed up at his cast. "That's just dumb. Dee—u—em."

"Compound," he said proudly, lifting it up as though to block a punch.

Herb came back across the tent, looking at me sweetly. "Know what BARF stands for?" he asked Jamie. A diesel engine rumbled loudly as it passed beyond the tent, drowning out the lively morning calls of the birds and the chimpanzees.

"Vomit . . ." Jamie said, stalling. "I guess. Or, like, upchuck."

"Biologically appropriate raw food." Mbele pronounced the words in his deep, mellifluous voice.

"How could barf be raw?" Jamie asked. He was very serious. "There's stomach acids, and don't they cook whatever's in your stomach?"

I lay back down, amused. I'd taught him how to make ceviche last summer with tiny scallops and even tinier shrimps. I'd told him that the acid in lime juice essentially "cooked" the seafood. He'd put two and two together, the acid in lime juice and the acid that digests food in a stomach. He was a lovely match for his uncle.

The last image I saw before closing my eyes was Mbele holding Jamie's fingers, the ones that protruded from his cast, and he seemed to be pressing them to see if they were swollen. Herb had Jamie in a headlock and was kissing him on the top of his head, and they were laughing. "How's the other guy look?" Herb asked. "He in a body cast?"

Hoarding

She now understands the Cat Woman, a staple of every neighborhood, the woman who lives alone with a dozen cats, or two dozen, the house sending up a reek that can be smelled from the sidewalk—this is a person she understands something about now, when perhaps she hadn't before. She does not like cats, has never liked cats, but widowhood redefined companionship, and so she has bees now, and mice, and possums and rats and squirrels and spiders, and she will not spray them into oblivion, or allow them to be sprayed into oblivion. She understands these new populations in her life, their industry, their nocturnal foraging, their quick and precise retreats into the undergrowth.

Beatrix Potter had depicted a widow: "Mrs. Tittlemouse was a most terribly tidy particular little mouse. . . ." Now she too was tidy and particular, and she understood a little how others thought of her, as she too had been taught to hate old women, and getting old, and rats, their long gray tails like a grandmother's thin gray braid, and like a possum's tail . . .

but now they were all her great, busy company, and some nights she stood on the threshold of the back door, watching the huge garden spider spin from the eave of the garage to the branches of the hibiscus, and the irregular lace gleamed in the pale light and she thought that perhaps she was a happy madam at the approach of night—at the approach of work!

And through the late evenings, as she reads, the possums move beyond her bedroom windows, their footsteps slow, significant. She will laugh sometimes and think "Are they chasing skirt out there?" She had first heard that phrase from a sheriff in Colorado one summer when she was six or seven. During the night there had been a prowler around the cabin, and her beautiful mother and her brother and she had listened as the footsteps crunched the pine needles, the slow progress around the back to where her mother's window was, and then the quiet for a long time; the giving-up or the talking-out-of or the gathering-of-a-plan-for-the-next-night ensued and the footsteps continued past the side windows and down the path through the pines to the dirt road along the stream. "I think I know who it was," the sheriff said to her mother the next morning, crushing his cigarette under the toe of his boot. "He's a real skirt chaser. He saw you at the gas station and asked around."

The prospect of running out of something seemed painful to her, quietly disastrous, as though too much else had run out in her life and so at least the cupboards might remain full. She was aware and yet not so much aware, because each day she needed some chore to do, or used the chore to get herself out of the house, to put herself among people, to somehow make herself feel busy, and she was busy, a professional, and yet that was it, she was busy *professionally*, a most terribly tidy professional, and what she did not have was a personal life. But just possibly, if the refrigerator were full, someone might come to dinner.

She was not much of a shopper or a pack rat, but this new quiet imperative set in, and well before she ran out, she stocked up again, coffee beans, for which she walked several blocks to a street of shops, to Graffeo's, and coffee filters. She would finish a box and buy another immediately, even though there were three more boxes in the cupboard, and tuna and capers and olive oil—to run out seemed some event she was staving off, keeping away from herself, and she went on eBay and found more Ball Mason jars, the old blue ones, and ordered them up and filled them with beans and lentils and grains, teff and amaranth and spelt. Rices, too. Who knew that when she needed there to be so many different kinds, so many different colors of rice, there would be? Himalayan red and Korean black and jasmine and basmati, and this in brown or white, entailing more blue jars, her larder full and detailed—

She walked the aisles in the store where she bought crackers and cheeses, and she pulled boxes of cheese straws off the shelves, both kinds, Parmesan and Cheddar, a good supply, though she had never opened a box just for herself, ever. Maybe they would come if she laid in provisions. Was that it? Preparations. For guests, should they drop in, guests on their way to the museums or the theater, the opera, provisions for that possibility, the chance that people might come, might visit, drop in, have a cheese straw, a glass of wine. The good high spirits of greeting, of being together after so long, such a thrill to see people, the world coming in at the gate, "Oh, did you hear . . ." and "Oh, that's a riot," and "Oh, this tastes so perfect, a little bite before *Lohrengrin;*

the set's supposed to be magnificent," but it took them so long to come, and then most times they didn't come, and the delightful provisions, the French cookies, the fancy crackers, sat high up in the cupboard. Now she suddenly knew what her grandmother had been waiting for, prepared for, a visit should someone have the time for an old woman, and she knew—suddenly she knew at the age of forty-seven—why the cookies were stale, so perfect, and stale.

It seemed important to have supplies, sugar and flour, ten-pound sacks, and boxes of matches; she bought sets of pot holders from the small hardware store that sold the dou-bled terry-cloth ones, and the larder had cans of tomatoes for sauces, and clams and olives, jams, jellies, honey. Some-one looking might think, Good, I'll survive here with the widow for a while if there's a major earthquake! But if the earth moved, she'd be alone, she knew that because, you know, the earth didn't move when you were a widow, and she would laugh a little at this. She knew she'd be alone, and that there wouldn't be any gas for the stove and that her supplies were not of the kind recommended, but she wouldn't spend a penny on dehydrated food or any of those items manufac-tured and marketed for calamity. She hoarded comfort, and if the other came, it seemed more familiar than not, and how much different would her life be anyway, all moved into one room, her bed piled with all the quilts in the entire house and the front door bolted and wedged with a chair and the windows, which were no longer windows but gaping holes, covered over with cardboard. For a time there might be the quiet hiss of the gas, but she would go to the source and shut it off, and she knew the shut-off for the water, too. She knew not to make it worse, not to open the valves, but, rather, to close them off—and she moved her hand, incanting, "Righty tighty, lefty loosey." She knew all about closing the world out, shutting it down, occluding access.

Conversely, she'd known for some time that if she wanted any kind of a social life, she would have to make it, that invitations extended her way were few, and then, because she was out of practice socially, she wasn't ever quite sparkling enough or important enough to invite again, or often. She didn't have much anger or consternation over this, though she was sad too often now, and not much given to laughter as she once had been. Once, laughter had been a currency to her, something she cherished and banked, sounds she loved hearing, and so sometimes now she extended invitations just so that she could hear laughter in the house. She ordered lamb shoulder from her butcher and bought Israeli couscous in the one store where she could find it, though still it wasn't the right kind; she reduced *vin santo* down in a small pan and mixed it with oil for the salad; she baked a chocolate cherry torte. There would be lamb stew with garlic and baby lima beans, and this laddled over buttered couscous, and a salad with asparagus and toasted almonds and sliced grapes. She was ready for them, had pulled the cork on a Burgundy and had laid out *bunderfleisch* with little onions and cheese straws—no one would starve, she used to say, and people used to laugh to hear her say it, knowing that no one had ever left this house hungry—she used to be so proud of these things, and fully aware, too, that people maybe went home and said snotty things about her, about the food, but maybe not, too; she was the unreliable narrator of her life now, or just quietly, dazedly witless about it. She didn't know; she just didn't know. She wanted people here, wanted to hear conversation and laughter, but then, it was so hard to do everything alone, and even before people arrived, she grew worried, and then more tired because she had not been the entertaining one, the one who told stories and made everyone laugh, and so could she feed people and keep the conversation going if she had to? . . . And then sometimes a friend would come join her in the kitchen and would ask how she was, "No, really, how are you?" and this question was so hard to deflect because it was someone asking who cared and who wanted an honest answer, but she was setting out the salad on the plates or making sure the couscous didn't overcook, and so her answers could only be perfunctory or a little bit blithe, a sampler motto or a bit of pioneer wisdom, the "one day at a time," "do what you can," "lemonade from lemons" kind of verbiage that she was grateful for, the sentences she could do chin-ups on as her feet dangled in the black well.

How was she?

But the salad just right and the parsley chopped or the couscous forked with butter—these were all bars she could sustain herself from, too, chin-ups, the chore that allowed her to lift herself, to do something that might actually result in someone being fed a good meal—an action with a result, the opposite of anything she might do in response to death, death with its mute pervasive brutality everywhere and nowhere.

The front bell rang and they stood behind the wrought-iron gate and called through the courtyard to her and she was happy to see them with their flowers and their bottles of wine and their expectant faces, and she was delighted to see them and exhausted—

At a meeting of her book group, an iPhone got passed around the table with a program on it—an app—that distorted people's faces, a miniature fun-house mirror, and when it was handed to her, she glanced briefly and passed it along. Her face was already a distortion to her, her entire life a distortion, and wasn't there a book to talk about, but really, truthfully, she did not care about the talking so much as she just wanted to be there within human company, but then she didn't want to be there, either, and who needed hand-held distortion when one's entire heart was amorphous?

Maybe she could say to people when they asked her how she was was that she wanted to laugh.

"Say something funny!"

Could she respond like that? She wasn't sure. Sometimes, when she'd invited people and they were coming, she'd start worrying, and she'd collect a few topics in her mind to bring up, or funny things in the news, but then it seemed it was yesterday's news and it wasn't as funny to them as it had been to her, or they knew what they thought already and she had to catch up, or admit that she hadn't heard that part of the story, and so how she was was out of it, behind the times, side-lined. Just this morning, the BBC News informed her that the prudent Swiss had developed a condom for teenaged boys, sized for teenaged boys, and she had laughed, thinking that would be one hell of a thing to try to sell, condoms for the small penis! She didn't envy the advertising agency that got that gig! The newscaster in his immaculate British accent went on to talk about these specially sized condoms called "the Hotshot," and she'd laughed again, thinking that was a pretty brilliant name with a beautiful double meaning, and maybe even a triple meaning, though she doubted teenagers knew what a "money shot" was, but maybe so. It was interesting what younger people knew these days, interesting how much pornography they'd seen, though even then, knowing what a money shot was as opposed to having merely seen it a hundred times?

She hadn't known the phrase until she was in her late twenties, and he had taught it to her—they were graduate students together—and sure enough, watching the films, there was always the money shot, the white ejaculate across the breasts or the ass or streaked across pubic hair.

He had been reading a book whose title after the snake eyes read *Hard Core: Power, Pleasure, and the "Frenzy of the Visible,"* because every English department in the country suddenly had Porn Studies, and he regaled her one early morning, telling tales of the bachelor party the evening before where there had been an unsettling amount of analysis as the films played, and she had been delighted. No one made her laugh like he did.

So she tried it out in the front room, wine poured and people settled and cheese straws and crudités offered. "Did you hear what the Swiss have come up with?" and after telling that part, she tried what was the funny part to her, the marketing nightmare, but it all fell flat and she sort of had to explain that she didn't think men, young or old, were going to line up to buy something that underscored the reality of their small penises, and one of her guests, a high school teacher, said she didn't really think young men worried about penis size anymore. "Oh," she said, "really?" and she heard Samuel Johnson's comment in her mind: "He was not only dull himself, he was the cause of dullness in others."

And so she would lose her nerve and eveything would seem so hard, and in the mid-day light nothing would be moving except her bees, but then she'd push herself and the nail driven into the rubber strip hanging off the garage door went in easily and straight and held, and she would deride herself and say, See, stop thinking everything's a peace agreement between the Israelis and the Palestinians—the garage door is fixed. But it took a lot of talking to herself, too much, and if she hadn't had Oscar to clean the house or Daniel to tend the garden, her house would tell on her, would say, See, she's going downhill, and fast. She liked the expression "keeping up appearances," and certainly she'd been raised within a version of that, not that you cared what other people looked like, or what they had, but that you carried a standard all your own and exemplary. Her brother used to tease her, claim he wasn't taking her antiquing with him because she "looked like a million bucks" and no one gave him good prices then. Of course, he was out-and-out shameless in his bargaining and she always ended up feeling sorry for the dealers, thinking they had to make a living, too! But she didn't look like a million bucks any longer, if she ever had, and her appearance was a struggle, too, her hair graying so around her face and the various dye jobs so obviously what they were, no matter what they cost. She let more and more time go by between trips to the salon. What about just letting it go gray? was an incantation starting in the fifth week, and then in the sixth, and she liked these soft gray days, but sometime during the eighth week she relented and called and made an appointment with the surly Iranian man whose wife did her hair. On the phone he would say, "Yes, yes, I know you," and that would be it. She knew it would not be so difficult for her if he didn't answer the phone, or take the money afterward. When it was time to pay, he left his couch and the two television screens at the back of the salon and came to the front desk. He quickly palmed the bill she handed him for a tip, did not smile, and mumbled a

"Thank you" so resentful, it startled her the first time she heard it. Part of her resistance to having her hair done was wondering if her tip ever got to her stylist, his wife.

She drove a lot, living in Los Angeles, and she heard on the radio one day the results of a study done on whether or not old people smelled or began to smell more as they aged, the body undergoing some chemical process or degeneration. Did this aging process smell? No, was the answer researchers had found. No, older people did not smell more than young people; it was all a myth, rubbish, the noses of the young making something up. She shook her head inside the glass-and-metal capsule of her car—she shook her head. We smell of longing, she thought; we smell of desire; we smell of how unseemly these desires are at our age, and she struggled with herself a bit, said, You're not really old. Not really. But she was, too, in many respects, and what did it matter the age, the number, because her heart was weak and painful in her chest, and then she argued with herself some more, said, *The heart's a metaphor*, but that wasn't true anymore, either. Scientists— bless them—had found cells in the heart, cells with memory, they theorized, because heart-transplant patients were some-how taking on the characteristics of their heart donors, sud-denly wanting to ride fast motorcycles or eat buckets of pasta, something they had never cared for before, a dish their heart donor adored. Of course the heart had memory cells—this was undeniable; the heart was a great hoarder—and every time she thought of him, hers would seize and ache.

In the mornings, there was the mourning dove mak-ing her—or perhaps his—quiet quivering sounds, and she said, "Hello, how are you this morning?" and she waited, watching this perfect smooth football of a bird roost in the mint . . . and then she'd say, "I know, me, too," and they were quiet together, the dove settling even further within his—or her—feathers.

And in the mornings, too, the squirrels knitted, and she watched through the mullions of the dining room window their perfectly dexterous hands work back and forth, to and fro. Oh, she thought, if I could only get some yarn into those active hands, a pair of tiny needles, what fine scarves they would wear and how superior the hats as they leaped along the elm branches, the knitted pompoms flying beyond—

Occasionally people coming into the front courtyard would comment on her squirrels, how tame they were, how interested, and she would say, "Oh yes, those are my knitters," and she did not explain.

Nor did she explain how he had died when people asked who did not know. She did not attempt to describe the blood-brain barrier, what got past, what did not, what drug set up a competition and prevented what was necessary for a brain's health. She did not explain what pharmaceutical scientists knew but kept to themselves, pacing, alone, proprietary in their lifeless laboratories.

She thinks always now about the tall black man dressed in slacks and a beautiful V-necked sweater of fine thin wool, his elegant stride as he moved down the sidewalk. She watched from her kitchen window, which looks out on the street that divides Beverly Hills from Los Angeles. She watched the look of disgust build on his face as he saw the parking ticket on his windshield. He pulled his money clip from his front pocket and peeled off a bill with his long fingers and threw it into the bushes. He stood for moment gazing down the street, looking into the distance, and then he crossed the grass apron, pulled the ticket from beneath the windshield wipers and got into his car and drove away.

Had she really seen what she had just seen?

It took her a few moments to pull on clothes, sweat-shirt, jeans, Dr. Scholl's, but then she passed out the side door of her house and down the stairs and across the street and sure enough, suspended in the hedge was a one-dollar bill like a tiny hammock. She left it there, of course. She wasn't touching his voodoo or mojo or gris-gris or whatever badness he paid off, but she amused herself crossing the street back to her house thinking, Yeah, if it had been a one-hundred-dollar bill, would you have left it to do its hexing? But she would have. She had enough New Orleans in her, enough Martinique, to know you didn't mess with charms like that, with responses that called out the obvious bullshit of the world. You want to fine people fifty bucks because they left a car for ten more minutes on a city street, then great, let's call your greed for what it is. Here, have a little more, you greedy fucks. Sure, she'd leave it there if it were a thousand dollars!

The one-dollar bill in the hedge across the street lasted for a day. After all, there were gardeners and children from the various schools filing past, but for her, standing in her kitchen window, leaning against the sink, having her coffee, or pulling herbs and garlic from the basket on the sill—she knew the lucre was still there, suspended, torn into sturdy strips and woven into a nest by the birds or the squirrels or the possums, a hedge against the world's nastiness, and she took her lesson, too.

The Legal Case

❖

The young woman knows of a legal case involving an ex-husband who intercepts his former wife on a winding mountain road. They have been divorced by some type of official decree and the woman resides now with another man. She is carrying this new man's child; the ex-husband says something to the effect of, "I've heard you're pregnant. You sure are. I'm going to stomp it out of you." He rams his knee into her belly; the baby is born with a crushed skull—is born dead.

The ex-husband is let off the charge of murder because the law, or the way the penal code was written in 1872, didn't expressly state that killing a fetus in this manner was criminal behavior, feticide being distinguished from abortion, being an entirely different thing and not illegal in 1872. Why?

Because there is the more important issue, the dispositive question of whether or not the fetus was a human being on February 23rd, 1969. "Murder" is the unlawful killing of a human being, and in the legislature of 1850, "human being" had the settled common-law meaning of a person who had been born alive.

Advances in medical science have redefined what a live or viable human being is, but not before February 23rd, 1969, when a man kneed the fetus in his ex-wife's belly, had the law managed to redefine its terms. The ex-husband could not be convicted of murder by a law that would not convict him of murder, let alone convict him of feticide, which wasn't a crime.

The young woman understood that the judge, the counsel, the court could call "stomping" a fetus "out" of a woman's belly a crime, but that because it was not enumerated in the statute, it could not be punished under that statute. We could all agree a crime had taken place, but if the law didn't enumerate it, the law as it existed could not be used to convict.

The young woman wonders if she could sit here now in this café with pencil and paper and come up with every possible example of criminal behavior surrounding women and men and unborn fetuses, wonders if even the most brilliantly generative minds could ever possibly meet with law what the real world serves up? She decides she must try, though, because every horrible scenario she can come up with would then be covered by the law. Wouldn't—if her mind were particularly generative—the law have broader and broader scope, wouldn't there be fewer and fewer crimes that the law didn't cover? If she could make her mind so utterly contemptible, so hatefully imaginative, wouldn't she have done the world a great service? Wouldn't there be fewer crimes the law didn't cover, fewer crimes for the world to surprise us with?

Before she even begins to move her pencil along the page, she is reminded of Zeno's Paradox, her mind implying that she will never actually achieve comprehensive law, will never actually quite get there; and she is reminded also of Occam's razor, that "entities are not to be multiplied beyond necessity," and she sees a pregnant belly sliced so methodically, so finely, so many times from breasts to *mons veneris* that the fetus is born through gills—her imagination is a tremendous lack of consolation in the face of the world's vast store of unimaginable events that happen every day. Just then, she is distracted by a couple at the front of the café.

The man props his foot on the spindle of the café chair and thus his knee comes to just below his chin because he is leaning forward toward a woman he finds enthralling. The young woman watching can read this from every momentary tableau the man folds into, folds out of, his foot finding its way back to the floor, his back even more tilted toward his wife, he is animate with love of her, his arms now laid across the table, both palms resting open right beneath her face, his head lifted to her, smiling, talking through the smile, his words continuous, his body is draped across the table to her, but now instantly rampant, he is talking to the waiter, ordering something, the young woman watching cannot tell as yet what? the waiter vanishes, and the man's shoulders swoop down again toward the table and he rests his head on his arm, but then he raises his head and brings the hand of that arm and tucks it beneath his ear so that he's now resting on an elbow, talking the entire time, his eyes cast out toward the street, then at her, a finger stiffening from his other hand, pointing, she is laughing, accused, and the finger waggles a bit in the air and his foot is once again propped on the chair rung, his knee up close to his chin, close to her belly, they are seated so near to each other, they are both laughing, and his body straightens slowly, quickly, like time-lapse photography, a flower stalk emerging up out of the ground, sword-shaped leaves flaring away from the stalk, shooting outward, the flower bud forming furled, now unfurling, blossoming, his body is so completely in thrall to hers, the fine camber of pregnancy beneath her white trapeze dress a pearl within the bivalve which is both their bodies, a desire so physically realized, he can barely keep himself from the appetite that is his life with her, now, in these days, a hunger so happily hunger, an oh God yes in every conjugation of his body again and again

and again,

it is, it is becoming, it will be,

he is in her body, he has not touched her once, though all his body is of one verb, the young woman watching can see this, one verb.

The young woman watching cannot take her eyes from this scene in the café. Battering at it from every angle is the legal case.

Keeler v. Superior Court
Supreme Court of California
2 Cal. 3d 619, 470 P.2d 617 (1970)

[Five months after obtaining an interlocutory decree of divorce, a husband intercepted his wife on a mountain road. She was in an advanced state of pregnancy by another man; fetal movements had already been observed by her and her obstetrician. Her husband said to her, "I hear you're pregnant," glanced at her body and added, "You sure are. I'm going to stomp it out of you." He shoved his knee into her abdomen and struck her. The fetus was delivered stillborn, its head fractured.]

That is the actual wording of the case. The young woman thinks of the mountain road, of what it means or does not mean, of how evocative it is of isolation, or perhaps of something else? Is it legal coding for a certain class of people? Or a certain area where there is a certain class of people? And there are other curiosities. There is the first decree, the interlocutory decree of divorce, which, if you read the grammar of the sentence, the husband has asked for and received, and then the second decree: "I'm going to stomp it out of you." You see, you see, all the verbs are wrong. He got his divorce; he can't also stomp out his ex-wife's future children. He can and he does and, even more strangely, he uses his knee as a foot, the knee remade into foot, or was it the verb remade?

And what of these last words, "its head fractured"? This peculiar wording—do heads fracture or get fractured? Don't we say a fractured skull? A broken head having almost a cartoonish benignity like "Hey, you're busting my chops," said in a Bugs Bunny voice. So many words all wrong—and most cruelly the law worded in such a way that neither the word *crime* nor the act to which it is referent mean anything at all.

Breathe

❖

She moves the temperature dial on the iron to Linen, the setting farthest from Off, and almost as far from all the Ons: Rayon, Nylon, Dacron, Orlon, those edgy snarling fabrics pressed smoother by a body wearing them than by any iron, fabrics instantly aromatic of a body's heat, of sweat and nerves, last night's alcohol, even of some recent influenza not yet quite purged. Next to the Ons live the Els and the Tates: Acetate and Triacetate near Arnel and Kodel and Dynel, but up on the hill live Cotton and Linen, vast estates requiring serious maintenance. The young woman does not know what to think about the socioeconomics of her iron's temperature gauge, the tepid, tightly crowded housing tracts, so many she passes through before the hot-blooded Kentucky horse farms of Linen and Cotton.

She has made it up, she supposes, insisted on the metaphor, and yet it is the clerk at Macy's who pigeonholes her when she is surprised that Macy's no longer carries any 100 percent cotton or linen table coverings. "Don't shop at

Macy's much, huh?" he says. Live up on the hill, shop at Neiman Marcus, Saks Fifth Avenue; it is all over his face how he thinks of her, what he thinks of her, that somehow and in some absolute way linen and cotton are now the province of the rich.

The iron cracks quietly, once and then again, breathing now, emanating heat as though fed a good soup. She likes its company.

She listens to the telephone ring, its shrill marmishness. She waits for it to stop, for the mincing snips and grinds of the answering tape.

Furled within the white enamel drum of the washing machine, wrung of water but still wet, are the cloth and napkins for tonight's dinner. The cloth is Irish flax, hemstitched, pink. The napkins are Italian, huge, deeper in color, a color as luscious as dog tongue. She has bought it all from flea markets. She extracts a napkin from the heavy rope of laundry, shakes it out, and settles two corners on the ironing board, the other two corners dropping down toward the carpet. The iron pulls against the linen, pleating a corner into a fan; the iron is not yet hot enough. She shakes the napkin out again and spreads it flat against the board. His insistent voice comes over the speaker: "Pick up. I know you're there."

Pause, a pause within which the iron cracks three times, and steam blows from the holes in its soleplate. He is breathing, too, waiting. She listens. She envisions his face. He has a marvelous nose, as big as a doorknocker; no, she is being fanciflul, but certainly it sits upon his face as beautifully as a good piece of bronze on a chancellery door. She is distracting herself from his insistence—his nose is a lion, a twisting fish, a long-fingered hand with a diamond ring—

"Ikie, is that a diamond on your nose?"

"'Tis snot!"—distracting herself because she thinks she will not *pick up*, as his voice commands her to do, thinks this not maliciously, not particularly peevishly, either, but, rather, just thinks that she will think this for such a time as will allow a small refusal to operate. She loves him enough that occasionally, very occasionally, she must refuse him, must take herself away from his needs and desires and hold herself up before herself, must find where seams have frayed, buttons cracked, must smooth away the wrinkles and pattern once again how she fits within herself.

"Hmm," he says on the answering tape, "I could have sworn you were there."

As he talks, she hunkers down and reties the drawstring of the ironing board's cover, double-knots it, tucks the ends neatly up into the narrow metal trussing. The iron totters a bit on the board as she does this, and, looking up, she imagines it tumbling down, becoming a griddle across her face, burning the bridge of her nose, her left cheek, scorching an ear.

She straightens up.

The iron breathes.

He breathes on the answering machine, sighs, and then it is just the iron sighing.

She sees the taut skin of her grandmother, the scar tissue covering her arms and legs, the scars drawn tight, like bread dough stretched across limbs. In the days of incinerators, when everyone burned their garbage, sparks had escaped through the heavy screen, and there was just enough pitch in the pine needles so that in her grandmother's first glance out the small window of the summer cabin, the pines wuthered quietly, but in the next—conflagration. What her grandmother thought she could stop with a bucket of water, no one ever knew, but why so much scarring, why over 50 percent of her body seared of its skin? The dress, nylon jersey, so new, so chic, her grandfather's delight in his wife's good figure even after so many years, the dress melting at a lower temperature than cotton would have, than wool, those threads reserved for the fighting men, for a military that knew about bodies burned alive, incendiaries, cockpits set aflame—give those men a chance to get out, to roll upon the ground, to find water, the natural fabrics not such a ready searing suit of glue that only molded itself to the body hotter and hotter—

The young woman cannot come to love these newfangled fabrics, new before she was born, a war effort.

No matter these fabrics take such little time, such little care—though that is the entire matter: They take such little care.

She irons square after square and then the big rectangle.

Now they can all come. To dinner. And she will answer to him, too. And small expanses of cloth that she has smoothed of wrinkles and then creased neatly into quadrants can be spread with her guests' fingertips, can now travel from their laps to their lips, and what she likes and is sure of is that they would never think, as they lift these linen squares, that she has pressed each one expressly for them, the first kiss she gives a little hard, a little stiff, but then, as they eat, they are kissing back and she is kissing them over and over again—and what she likes most and is most sure they never calculate is how often they kiss her labors through the evening—oh, her work is kissed over and over. How they love what she irons, how they anoint these flaxen threads with their mouths—

Later, the house not yet quiet, though emptied, she fills the washing machine with water, surfactants, nonchlorine bleach, detergent, and baking soda, and, holding up the first napkin, she sees all their kisses once again. How much they loved the sauce with veal stock and mushrooms, the strawberry tarte, the good zinfandel!

She could never think of bringing violence to their faces—even if it is just in her mind—the synthetic cloth melting across their eyes and mouths. Their faces, their entire skin—it is a type of innocence shrouding their bodies—its care is sacred to her.

In an Anita Desai novel she read last year, there are two distinct versions of a woman's death. In the first version, she rises early in the morning, before light, removes her "cotton clothing," wraps a nylon sari about her, knotting it at the neck and knees. She pours kerosene over herself and sets herself on fire. In the second version, the one the neighbors and servants claim, the woman's husband and mother-in-law drag her from bed, make her remove her cotton clothing, tie her up in a nylon sari, pour kerosene over her, and set her on fire. Both versions have the detail of the nylon sari exchanged for cotton, and the whimpering charred bodydying slowly.

The young woman leans against the metal coldness of the machine, thinking about this novel, *Fasting, Feasting*, waiting for the swush and whirl to have swushed and whirled enough so that she can turn the machine off and go to bed and sleep while these linens soak. In the mounting, preternatural whiteness of the suds agitating, she sees her cousin the naval flier in dress whites, a lieutenant. They stand outside a funeral home. Their grandmother had not died from her burns, but she is dead now, years later, and they are talking after the memorial. Why this other subject comes up, the young woman does not remember, but probably because her cousin looks so starched, so fresh, and probably because she reaches out to feel the fabric, understands it immediately to be synthetic. "But your flight suits, they're cotton, yes?" she asks. "They mustn't be synthetic," she almost begs.

"No," he says, but then he tells her about naval twill, that dress whites used to be 100 percent cotton, as did all the whites onboard the carriers, the cloth for the sailors, the enlisted men, and, yes, he says, yes, they know, it is not half as safe; they know this new naval twill will burn far more rapidly, will become hot plastic on bare skin, the enlisted men, they know, but it is the cost, the labor of cotton.

The Neiman Marcus, Saks Fifth Avenue of cotton? she wonders.

On her bedside table, as she stands waiting for the washing machine, a book titled *American Plastic: A Cultural History* awaits her. She has wanted to understand her cousin's information more, has wanted to map the relationship between war and the production of nylon. She surmises that her sense of its chronology is inherited and perhaps not accurate. She even assumes that her sense of nylon's penchant for violence is idiosyncratic.

In her reading, what moors her attention is the early press on nylon and how it centered on one word, *cadaverine*, a nitrogenous material derived from human corpses. *The Washington News*, "basing its observation on an interpretation of the patent," suggested that "one of the ways to prepare the new synthetic silk fiber might be to make it out of human corpses by using cadaverine, a foul-smelling chemical substance formed during putrefaction, after burial."

DuPont's spokespersons, keeping their public's eye on the prize—silk-like hosiery strong as steel—kept evading this press by repeating the mantra "coal, air, water; coal, air, water," because cadaverine could be gotten from a sticky black tar formed as coal is heated. Coal, air, water: better things for better living through chemistry.

Indeed, so clamorous were women for hosiery of any kind—those were the war years—that, cadaverine or no, women fervently embraced the possibility of synthetic silk. "No More Runs, stockings as hard as steel" was, the young woman understands, pretty much a complete lie, but the fact of stockings at all during the war, no matter their threads, no matter that the exhaust from a car or a bus could burn them right off women's legs—and often did. No matter.

She learns that also of seemingly little note to women was the suicide of nylon's inventor twenty days after he applied for the patent. *The Washington News* suggested that the inventor, Wallace Hume Carothers, "had been consumed by his own invention."

Finally, sitting up in bed, the house quiet, the washing machine quiet, the table linens soaking, he breathing beside her, the young woman reads that even nylon came to be used up by the war, that after DuPont had hooked women on "nylons," that even those were taken for the manufacture of tires, glider tow ropes, cargo parachutes, machine-gun parts. Papers ran photos of women plunked down on sidewalks, stripping their legs, "Sending Their Nylons Off to War" and "Taking 'Em Off for Uncle Sam."

He sighs and casts a heavy arm out across her legs. Come to sleep, this arm is saying to her, come breathe beside me. But she thinks of this word, *cadaverine*, and she cannot shake it, this late-night mantra, cadaverine, that which is corpse-like, cadaverine, the source of nylon, the fabric that does not breathe.

Burqa

❖

The dog lay heavy and quiet at the foot of the bed, asleep still. What on earth? It had been a progression of sound, a distinctly audible slithering, a loud whoosh, and then a quiet scatter. The woman raised her head, looking not toward the door, but toward where she'd heard the puzzling commotion, the tremendous full band of New York City just beyond the windows, blindered, though hung also with panels of pale green cloth. She looked into the greenish penumbra-ed light. There was no one.

The apartment was new to her, a one-bedroom, because now he schooled in California, and today it was his birthday, September 5th. She had carried him inside her in a cab this day nineteen years ago, past the clock on Grand Central Station, past the yellow arrow that said "This Way," pointing uptown traffic to the right, as though all of New York was helping to bring this boy into the world, "This Way" to Lenox Hill Hospital, nineteen years ago. Almost a cliché, she thought, the hugely pregnant woman in a speeding taxi, the cabbie glancing into the backseat nervously—Oh shit, don't have that kid in my cab, oh shit—and yet the driving gentler, respectful of its cargo in a way it usually wasn't.

"Lenox Hill, right?" he kept asking, "Seventy-seventh and Lex, right?" as though he'd never driven New York before. "A boy, yeah, really? Amazing what they can tell you nowadays—we're halfway there," but there had really been no rush, and the doctors had sent her away, to walk the shops on Madison Avenue, block after block to bring on a centimeter, and then another and another, until there were nine centimeters, that mythic distance.

She'd have to make sense of this sound she'd heard in her new bedroom, but out of the corner of her eye she saw the telephone, and she calculated what time it was on that far coast and when she could call him, her beautiful boy.

How many parties there had been for him, the big, over-the-top ones, with several boys and their parents, the brownstone ravished with noise and glee and the sound of glasses and music and shouts and Jack barking, joyous over so much boyish company, and the small parties at Villa Mosconi's in the Village, two or three boys and their pal, her son, and she would think even then, so many years into his childhood, in the charming noise of that restaurant, she would think of her body on that day he was born, and on the days leading up, her terror, day in, day out, the word "miscarry" so blaming, "*she* miscarried," so personally inditing, but no woman did the mis-carrying as a fetus fell from her, no woman controlled that . . . and yet the language, goddamn the language, and just yesterday she had been standing, holding her flowers at the bodega on Second, waiting to hand the Korean man her money, and the young couple in front of her buying alstroemeria were laughing and the girl said sagely, "You're born alone; you die alone."

She watched them as they walked away into the urban sunlight, two lithe figures in the prime of their stupidity. No, no, she did not hate young people, but she did depend on them not to accept the status quo, not to traffic in the language of their elders; she depended on them for their energies, their force in the world, their revolutions, and yet here was the oldest misogyny, that we somehow came into the world without a mother's body accompanying us into being on a pillow of her own blood.

She had handed her white lilies to the Korean man. He wrapped them carefully in a cone of brown paper, saying, "Very pretty, Casa Blancas, very pretty, usually buy roses," and yes, she did usually buy roses, and when they began to wilt, she tied them in bunches to dry. But the lilies were a difference to mark a difference, and here the lilies were now, even prettier, standing tall and just opening their long white petals in a vase near the phone. The pale green light of her bedroom surrounded her, and it was just kind enough that she could see her son's picture in its dark frame. Waves crashed on a beach as he strode out of the surf, his surfboard spanning his hips. She had now sent him off to another coast—or rather, he had wanted this vast distance—but nineteen years ago today, she had been there, around him, her arms and legs and lips around him, with him, so simply with him. Indeed, she had been his society and his source. He had not been born alone.

What could that noise have been? What was that long slither and whoosh and scatter that had woken her but not the dog? She turned her head now and looked up at the ceiling, its fresh paint. So many shades of pale in the early morning light, as though she were looking through veils.

She had seen something once in Saudi Arabia, a public square between two museums, a huge courtyard, and dozens of women completely veiled in black with their children, but a little boy was running from one black shroud to another black shroud, screaming with fear and anguish, and finally a woman had stepped out in front of him and lifted her veil just enough so that he could see it was she, his own mother or keeper or guardian, whoever this completely shrouded woman was to him, She, finally She had stepped out and lifted the veil so that he could know that he was safe.

The woman thought of this scene. She thought of the trauma of removing the mother's face from her children in public places where a kind of occular home was most needed. But she had sent her own son to boarding school for a time, and perhaps that had been a mistake for him, for her? She did not know.

She turned her head again and looked toward the windows. What had that sound been? She nudged the dog with her foot and he rearranged himself within his deep sleep. "You are useless," she said quietly to him, to her lovely knight of a dog, an English springer spaniel, but then she thought not so quietly that she was useless now, too, fifty-eight, disappeared into a small apartment with veiled light.

She had been a wonderful gardener, or at least she had attempted to be, and the garden at the brownstone had been lush, emergent, laid out classically, and growing into stateliness. Why was she thinking of her garden, and of all the work she had done? Perhaps of all the cooking she had done, too, of how many people she had fed in her lifetime of jolly tables, and of her child, of feeding him, keeping off that wolf of a phrase, "failure to thrive." But he had thrived—they all had thrived—and she had tended gardens, had fed people, and when her divorce had happened, the same people who had eaten so lavishly at her table had just as lavishly taken sides or found other tables, and it had crushed her, their ease at defection.

It was true, she usually did buy roses from the careful Korean man, and usually two dozen of one color, a small monopoly, and when the roses started to wilt, she tied them in bunches with raffia and hung them upside-down to dry. Several dried bouquets hung from the top of her bookcase, not yet filled with books, and when it was still too early to call, she walked to the windows to draw the curtains, and then looking she saw what had fallen, and the floor was like a stage strewn with roses, the roses thrown for a diva or a prima ballerina at the end of a performance, Brava! Brava! the roses falling upon the stage, and these roses had made a dried scattering sound.

She liked that she could see in this what she saw, that her mind imagined art and performance and discipline and beauty—she had made so much beauty.

"You're born alone, you die alone."

Who was that solo act, that sui generis, that singular who had then hoodwinked entire civilizations with such stunning propaganda? At least she had made art, beauty, a boy's fine limbs.

Damned Spot

❖

For all the last years of my husband's life, we owned an English bull terrier named Damned Spot. He came from a white-and-black brindle line, Fidelis Sebastian of Silmaril, but he was completely white and looked almost exactly like Gen. George Patton's bull terrier. The name Damned Spot started out as a joke—a gag really, to get my husband's mother to swear—and as years went by, it became funnier and funnier to hear Hilda saying in her sweet Arkansas accent, "Now, Damned Spot—you stop that!" Damned Spot obliged us in this gag, as he would not respond to just the name Spot— though Hilda had tried this shortening many times—and when Damned Spot lived in Michigan and the ladies who worked for the vet there declined to use his full name, he would not budge an inch of his very muscular seventy pounds when it was his time with the doctor. He stood his ground like a marble table, his tongue lolling out, his teeth in a crazed smile. I hesitate to suggest there was cognition or intellection in his eyes—he was one of the dumbest dogs I ever met—but certainly one could read a kind of sentiment that went along the lines of Why don't those women stop making noise and pay some attention to me, ME, DAMNED SPOT?

Paul and I always relished saying to these staunch Michigan ladies, "You need to use his full name; he won't respond to just half of it," and he wouldn't, which was an almost endless source of amusement for us and one of the few arenas in which Damned Spot performed to our specifications. Bull terriers do very little that they do not wish to do, and they do even less of what you want them to, but Damned Spot seemed somehow at the vanguard of comedic excellence when it came to his name and his refusal to respond to just half of it. I realize, as I write this, that he was a bit of an artist, something I've failed to consider until now.

English bull terriers were created a couple of hundred years ago by crossing English bulldogs with an English white terrier now extinct. The breeder, James Hinks of Birmingham, wanted the broad chest of a bulldog but not the dwarfism in the limbs that makes bulldogs' legs bow. Bull terriers have a normal bone structure, perhaps even supernormal, as their legs are exceedingly straight, if not stiff. When Damned Spot barked, his front legs lifted off the ground as though he were a chair leaned back. I have heard some controversy over just what all else is in the breed—perhaps some dalmatian—but no matter what, they were originally bred for dogfighting, which is the point of their recessed eyes. In other words, it would be hard for an opposing dog to sink its teeth into them. Because of the phrase "dogfighting pit" and the dogs who were consigned there, bull terriers are often confused with pit bulls or the American Staffordshire terrier, but these are distinct breeds from bull terriers, with very different traits and personalities. Bull terriers are hugely affectionate and loyal, and one must read their strength within that context. I have often been thrown halfway across the kitchen by an affectionate nuzzle from Damned Spot, or moved entirely off the bed as he insinuated himself as close as he could possibly be. For years, I had to make sure the doors to the bathroom were closed when I drew a bath, because if they weren't, I would go into the bathroom and find Damned Spot, his eyes a bit glazed, luxuriating in a cloud of Kneipp herbal bath, juniper or almond blossom or spruce. Damned Spot loved his baths, and asking him nicely to get out of yours was to forget the hedonist you were addressing. Either you agreed to sidle yourself up along one side of the bathtub or you waited your turn.

Paul had originally wanted an English bulldog, but, being bookish people, we consulted—breeders, dog encyclopedias, veterinarians, owners—and what we encountered was information we did not love. Not only were bulldogs very expensive, most of them having to be born by Cesarean section because their heads had been bred to be so gigantean, but they were constantly at the vet's with dermatological issues, not the least being rashes that broke out within their neck folds. This chronic malady entailed applying Vaseline to the dog's neck twice a day, and years of prednisone, an expensive prescription as prescriptions go. Bulldogs were also known to be magnificent farters, and droolers, and rather stupid, and I looked at my husband with a kind of pleading in my eyes. How exactly English bull terriers came into the negotiations, I'm not sure, but we had friends who had relatives who knew breeders, and soon we were in conversation with a couple in Florida, the Cavanaughs. Fidelis Bull Terriers. We waited through one litter, and then a video arrived of a second litter, and puppy after puppy was put atop a short table in a fairly destroyed backyard for my husband to choose from. The Cavanaughs bickered at each other in the background, but all you could see of them were hands and an occasional profile. It was a strange video, an artifact of sorts, the pay dirt of documentarians, and though I did not see this video until well after Damned Spot had arrived in our lives—I was commuting from Los Angeles to Michigan at the time—I relished its weirdness: It took special people to love these canine insurgents enough to own them, but it took strangeness of a higher order to actually proliferate them on earth! The video captured much of this.

To lend a fuller sense of the general reception of bull terriers, I must tell you of a passage in a little-known John Fante novel in which a bull terrier is shot dead at point-blank range on a beach in Malibu, California. When I first read this passage, I did not—bull terrier owner that I was—reel back in my chair in surprise and anguish. Rather, I understood the sentiment precisely. That said, I admit that when Target discount stores launched their advertising campaign with a white bull terrier whose eye spot was instead a red target, I balked. An early name for bull terriers was "White Cavaliers," and indeed much in the behavior of these dogs is cavalier—and cavalier in the face of all that Western civilization holds dear—but that is much of their value, too, their irrepressibility, their one-dog insurgency. To keep a bull terrier in your sights, to make one the mascot of your commercial ambitions—or the target of your murderous rage—is understandable. They are indeed spectacular-looking, and spectacularly badly behaved. But if you know bull terriers at all, you know well that they will not submit to our uses—and this is a fine thing. Paul and I amused ourselves by gauging the destruction that one bull terrier loose in a

Target store would wreak; we thrilled to the hordes of protective mothers hurrying their children from the too-bright aisles of merchandise, and we debated the time it would take even an experienced bull terrier owner to capture her wildly careening pet and get him back on a leash. It might only be a matter of minutes, but bull terriers—being physicists, too—expand time to allow the utmost mayhem.

Because so few people have actually ever seen a bull terrier, Damned Spot often had celebrity status when he went places—and indeed, he loved to be photographed and would stand completely still, all vain attention while the cameras clicked. What he thought was going on is anyone's guess, but somewhere in the deep reaches of his DNA, he knew about pomp and circumstance; he knew about show. Certainly Elgar had written that music for him!

Sometimes people—and they would almost always be men—would know that Gen. George Patton had had a bull terrier named Willie, who was much beloved by Patton, but for the most part people have not seen English bull terriers in the flesh. Even fewer have been around them for any amount of time, as not many are silly enough with their lives to actually attempt to raise a bull terrier—it is virtually impossible to do so anyway. But the Budweiser beer ads with their bull terrier mascot were a constant and almost singular source of identification for people. "Hey," people would exclaim on seeing Damned Spot, "it's a Spuds MacKenzie dog!" And they would often go on to object, "But Spuds MacKenzie has a spot on his eye. Plus, he isn't overweight like your dog." I would—though not always patiently—explain that Spuds MacKenzie was a two-year-old female, not completely grown, and that full-grown male bull terriers were like this, and that Damned Spot was not overweight, though obviously he wasn't built for speed on the veldt, either!

Sometimes they backed slowly away from me.

It's hard to know where to start in relaying the story of an obedience course that taught me more humility than any one human being should have to simper within—and taught my dog absolutely nothing. Perhaps a starting place would be to tell about how each of the ten classes ended. The instructor, dressed in jungle fatigues—I kid you not; it was Michigan, and the Michigan Militia met rather too regularly in the Kalamazoo town square—the instructor would visit each owner and his or her pet and have a few words—and of course the retrievers sat there like they were getting fucking manicures—and the dog trainer would come to us, and come to us last—she knew about power—and she would look at me, and then she would look down at Damned Spot, his teeth bared in his characteristic crazed smile, his tongue lolling out, his paws planted foursquare, barking ecstatically, and then she would look up at me again, and she'd shake her head with dismay, and then she'd say with the most practiced derision, "Well, he *is* the happiest dog." "Oh fuck you" was on my lips every time—she was so smug! But, of course, it's not as if she was wrong. It's just that I hadn't come to obedience school to be reconfirmed in thoughts of my dog's profound idiocy—I knew that full well. This was a Benjy Compson among dogs, a real Lennie if ever there was one, and I needed help, not confirmation of a reality.

For the first two weeks, the instructor watched me be dragged around the large circle the dogs and dog owners formed, and then, at the start of the third class, she moseyed her green-and-brown self over, swinging what looked to be a linked torture device. "This," she stated importantly, "is power steering. I suggest you purchase one immediately." What she held out to me was a choke chain with spikes. I sputtered. "That's vicious," I finally managed to say. "I could never use such a collar."

"Hold your hand out," she commanded, and I did, and she wrapped the spiked collar around my hand and then constricted it, and the spikes were angled in such a way that they threatened but didn't actually impale. It felt horrible, grisly. I purchased one directly following class.

To sum up this obedience course, I'll tell you about the last class, the class wherein one's pet passes an exam—oh yes!—and one receives a certificate that one can frame should one so wish! This last class was perhaps the most formalized of glimmerings we had that Damned Spot would never, ever, not on your Nelly be a trained dog, but—and this is an interesting *but*—he'd be incorrigible like no other, and in this incorrigibility our love took root.

If you have ever been to doggy obedience school, you know the drill: the Sit; the Walk in a Circle, in which the dog heels perfectly, never pulling on the leash; the Down; and then the Three-Minute Down, in which the dog rests alertly for three minutes by your side. These simple tasks do not seem to be a problem for most dogs to learn, and the retrievers slide out the birth canal knowing how to execute them, but a three-minute anything is not in bull terrier DNA, believe me, and so we're all there lined up on this last auspicious day. Damned Spot has succeeded passably—I use that term loosely—in walking and sitting, et cetera, but now it's time for the Three-Minute Down. He *is* down, but I'd say at thirty seconds he bounds up laughing his fool head off barking away. *What are you asses all doing!?* he seems to be shouting to the others. I push on his back to get him down again, and he goes, but it's like trying to deflate a rock, and he's down for perhaps twenty seconds this time and then he's up for the finale and will not be put down, and he barks and barks until all of the nine other dogs—even the golden retrievers, I'm very, very, very proud to say—bound up barking, too. Happiness takes the day. Anarchy reigns.

We loved to tell the story of Damned Spot and the Stetson Chapel wedding, because no matter what, Damned Spot's irrepressibility always amused us, his refusal to do much that didn't strongly feed his most sybaritic impulses. He was a marvel of hedonism, a Falstaff of a dog, though of course it was no matter of conjecture as to whether he had Falstaff's wits—he didn't. Nonetheless, there was something completely marvelous in the hugeness of his spirit, and in Michigan, where we lived rather uncomfortably for three years, he was a singular source of happiness. Not even Michigan could get this dog down!

We had a house on the campus of Kalamazoo College, a beautiful little two-story brick house built in 1928. It was just down a sweet wooded path from the quad, which was a miniature of Monticello, or the University of Virginia, moreover. Stetson Chapel sat primly at the top of the quad, and though obviously not Monticello, it was quite lovely, with its Palladian windows and bell tower where students rang changes almost daily. Every weekend during the spring and summer, elegant weddings took place at Stetson Chapel.

We set out for a walk one day, and before we could lean down to clip on Damned Spot's leash, he shot down the path, looking back once to say, Watch this, you idiot parents of mine! (We were always so grateful he couldn't actually speak, as his physical articulations were stinging enough.)

He was bounding up the hill to Stetson Chapel, to a wedding party being photographed, a regiment of groomsmen and bridal attendants, but more specifically, Damned Spot was bounding for the bridal gown fanned out down the long, sloping terrace, a cathedral-length train extending on the grass three or four yards, and all Paul and I could see was a deliriously happy Damned Spot rolling himself onto that vastness of peau de soie. We were screaming our heads off at Damned Spot to stop, hurtling our bodies after him as fast as we could, knowing full well that he was not stopping for God nor money, treats nor estrus, and finally, at the last possible instant, the groom stepped out of the picture and down the hill the necessary three or four yards and reached out his hand and grabbed Damned Spot's collar and hoisted him into the air and away from his gorgeously attired bride. We were full of admiration for this young man. Gallantry was not dead—not as long as there were curs like our boy in the world! Plus, this groom had just saved us thousands of dollars; we had no doubt about this whatsoever. Plenty of tuxedoed moneybags were standing there with not one whit of amusement on their faces. Instead, you could see the dollar signs flashing in their eyes. It was so colossally clear, their thinking: You will pay for having ruined my daughter's wedding, my niece's wedding, my daughter-in-law's wedding. Conversely, Damned Spot was joyous at the prospect and could not understand why no fun was being had at this far too elegant and sedate affair. Once again, a sentiment was resident in his eyes. This time, it went something along the lines of: *Look, I match the bride. I'm dressed all in white, a little mud on my paws, but hey, basically dressed for sanctity!* The smile on his face was as crazed as it ever had been.

* * *

Extremity has a way of leading us to language, and Damned Spot—because he was the dog he was—garnered many nicknames: "Cowboy," "Spot Meister," "Piglet," "Shark Dog," this last because for a time in his youth, the most prolonged youth imaginable, he ate anything and everything he could snatch up with his beautiful white muzzle. In fact, Paul relished telling the story of Damned Spot's having a bowel movement on the sidewalk that rang with pennies, a sort of zoologic slot machine; our young nieces and nephews knew never to put money in their mouths. One morning in Michigan, after a particularly raucous New Year's party the night before, we heard an odd crashing and then a Morse code of thumps, and then silence for a time, and then another crashing and the *tap, tap, tap*. Struggling up through murky heads, we finally roused ourselves to tread downstairs and see what our boy was up to. We watched from the kitchen doorway as Damned Spot knocked champagne bottles over and then held their necks down, lapping up what few drops he could get. He had already done this with several beer bottles, but it took the heavier topple of champagne bottles to finally wake us. It had been a big party, and Damned Spot had availed himself of enough alcohol to spend the rest of the day significantly subdued. One of the world's more pathetic sights is a hungover bull terrier, but perhaps even more pathetic were his parents missing their darling thug, even for a day.

On Damned Spot's walks, small children would hunker their little diapered selves down and start petting him, and their mothers would ask what the nice doggy's name was, and we'd say it, and of course the children—having such aural fidelity—would repeat his name immediately, before their mothers could suggest an alternative or a shortening to Spot. We would crack up when little tiny children would stand on the sidewalk, waving their even tinier hands, hollering, "Bye, Damned Spot, bye!" And they always got his name right, and they never tried to shorten it or censor it or alter it in any way. God bless them. Paul and I always expected our niece or nephew to be sent home from school for cussing, when they had, in fact, merely been naming their aunt and uncle's dog. The precision of children is to be greatly admired.

Damned Spot's name, children using it—this all seemed like rather innocent corruption to us, but then, of course, there was the quite intentional allusion in Damned Spot's name to Shakespeare, to a guilt-addled Lady Macbeth wringing her hands: "Yet here's a spot. . . . Out, damn'd spot! out, I say!"

And so thus, of course, "damn'd spot" being a literary allusion somehow elevated it out of the gutter and onto the sidewalk of civility, if not into the edifices of high culture— kind of like where the pigeons roost. There was no end to the range of this dog's name, and of course the literary allusion was dead-on, completely mimetic, as Damned Spot had no spots, just as Lady Macbeth has no actual blood on her hands as she wrings them, and some people got this and found it pretty funny. And some people didn't and were like, "Uh, but your dog, it, like, has no spots? Why did you call him Damned Spot?" The best response to this was just to bend down and scoop up the beloved dog's dejectus, because if you stood there and explained, people's faces went into the "Just-what-you'd-expect-of-a-college-professor" look, and working one's way out of that straitjacket of a stereotype was impossible. Or if you said Damned Spot's having no spots was ironic, you might end up explaining to a fifty-year-old person what *ironic* meant.

* * *

There was blood in Damned Spot's life, as there was blood in his name. He had been in the house the day my husband committed suicide, or perhaps he had been in the yard, where my husband actually held the gun to his head and pulled the trigger. I did not know, nor did the detectives, as there was no blood on Damned Spot, though one morning about a year after Paul died, I got an answer—at least I thought it was an answer—to the question of where Damned Spot had been when it happened.

Most nights, I could not sleep through the night, and I wandered the house crying, and Damned Spot followed me, and sometimes when I had stood in a room too long without moving, he would bark at me, and I would lean down to him and hold him—he was so great to wrap your arms around, with his massive smooth chest—and then we would go back to bed. In order not to hear myself weeping, I covered my head in pillows, and this one night I slept very, very deeply, so deeply that by ten o'clock the next morning I was still asleep. I felt something nudging me frantically in the side. Damned Spot was standing by the bed, and then he leaped up onto the bed and continued to nudge me, over and over, and quite desperately, and I said something to him, but my face was still under pillows, and I was trying to wake up, and then I did finally wake up enough to pull the pillows from my face, and looking into Damned Spot's eyes was like looking into a pure distillation of terror. "Damned Spot, I'm okay," I said to him. "Hey, guy, it's all right. I'm okay." And I knew that Damned Spot had tried to wake Paul up that day as he lay in our backyard with a bullet through his temple. My husband had been prescribed a cholesterol-lowering drug by his doctor and he had dutifully taken it for nine months, the highest dosage on the market. The scientific literature linking low-serum cholesterol to decreased brain serotonin activity covered the dining room table. Damned Spot had lived these last eighteen months in a state of shock akin to my own, and he had sat on my feet as I read this literature about the connection between low cholesterol and suicide.

On August 22, 2005, I stood at the high stainless-steel table in the veterinarian's examining room as Damned Spot died. He was as beautiful as he had ever been, his profile against the white towel, his eyes as dark and impenetrable as Apache tears. Perhaps there had been a kind of brain cancer. There had definitely been fibrotic lung disease—I had X-rays of his chest—but of course he died that day from a lethal injection. He lived for a year and a half after my husband's death, and he had lived with a woman who could not breathe, who was often desperately distraught, a woman who clung to him sometimes as though we both were drowning. The vet said, looking up at the X-rays on the light board, "I've never seen fibrotic lung disease in this breed, and it's pretty rare in dogs at all. Cats get it, but this is quite unusual." But I knew immediately—and I'm not a very woo-woo person—I knew that Damned Spot had taken as much into his own body as he could. I had spent a year and a half gasping, struggling to breathe—it was as though my heart were constricting around my lungs—and I had passed out several times, once my head hitting down on the computer keyboard. I had no doubt whatsoever that this dog had absorbed as much as he could absorb from his mistress's grieving, that he had tried to take it into his own body.

When they were alive, I called them "my guys," "my white dogs," and now they both were contained in small boxes that when tilted made the sliding, pebbly sound of dirt scattering on a coffin.

ACKNOWLEDGMENTS

Let me begin by thanking the person who conceived of this book, Erika Goldman, and who then made it happen. She is a writers' editor; she listens to the work first, wants the work audible on its own terms, first. Which then makes her a gift to both readers and writers alike. My deepest gratitude and affection.

And to Elizabeth Tallent, always and forever more, my friend and teacher beyond measure, this writer's reader, this writer's writer. Desert island: Woolf and Tallent.

And my gratitude and admiration for Richard Wrangham, Harvard biological anthropologist, whose research I lifted whole out of his marvelous books *Catching Fire* and *Demonic Males*, and who met this "theft" with great good humor. "Gut," the story, is completely imagined, but the science inspired the fiction and so I dedicate it to Richard Wrangham in hopes that he will write many more books for those of us in other disciplines to read. Thank you not only for finding "another way," but for showing it to us all.

And to my friend Rhoda Huffey who, when I asked her to, made a house full of grieving people laugh. Thank you, darling, for all your humor over so many years.

And to Vicki Forman, whose strength and intelligence and kindness and humor guide me always.

And to Varley O'Connor, Susan Segal, Bruce McKay, Jayne Lewis, my toughest readers, thank you for the precious ore of your hearts and minds.

And to Geri Hartfield and Tim Connors, Michael Barsa and Kim Yuracko, friends to me of such patience and duration, my love always.

And to Andrew Tonkovich, who published me when no one else would; thank you is never adequate, and to Lisa Alvarez and Brett Hall Jones, Graces in the world.

And to Arielle Read, tissue of my heart, so profoundly she is a part of any health I have. I love you dearly.

And to James McMichael, my teacher and friend of so many years. I would not recognize my life, were you not there. Thank you.

And to my sister, Lynette, who takes the worst of me and through the alchemy of her love makes me better, always, gives me peace, always, inspires me, always.

And to Carol Muske Dukes, whose fierceness for the right causes is a lesson to us all, my love and respect abidingly.

And my love to Michael Ryan, extraordinary poet, extraordinary friend.

And to bj swanson and Mardi Mitchell. Cocktails, darlings! I adore you both.

And to Margaret Russett—my Miss Meggles—thank you for your courage, your generosity.

And to poetry, and to poets, and to Molly Bendall and Susan Davis and Colette La Bouff Atkinson. Much love.

And to Rebekah Davis Dillingham and Laura Packard Latiolais, such a bounty of sisters in my life. You sustain me.

And to Peggy Reavey and Tom Reavey, for painting and architecture and the world's greatest company. My love and admiration.

And to Patti and Wayne Buck for their unending nurture, my love and gratitude.

And to Peter and Jozelyn Davis for always remembering me, including me.

And to Bill Handley, whose bright eyes at my gate have sustained me through these years, and whose understanding and friendship and great good humor have buoyed me many a day. Promise me you will always do Gilda Radner and Madeline Kahn in the "Baba Wawa" interviews! I am laughing even now.

And to my precious brother Christopher Latiolais, whose care of me has been beyond measure, though I have felt every ounce of it in learning how to thrive again.

And to Mark Dillingham, whose beautiful food over these last years was the only food that tasted good to me, often the only food I could taste. Thank you.

And my affection and admiration always to Ron Carlson, Bear, who will find what's good in a piece of writing no matter where one has hung it in the camp!

And to Lynh Tran, without whom so much would just be a dismal mess. Thank you, darling, for your fine wits, and for your bemused calm. You must teach me that last someday.

And much, much appreciation to the Ucross Foundation for the simple and profoundly realized colony within which they nurture so many artists.

And my gratitude and awe for Leslie Hodgkins, who ordered with such a fine ear the pieces in this collection—thank you—and who I am sure did a thousand other good turns to insure the publishing of this book.

And to Carol Edwards, a copy editor who reads not for orthodoxy, but for aesthetic, for sense, and for the sense of the aesthetic. Then she makes *that* better. Bless you.

And to Erika Goldman, again, and always, for changing my life, for giving me ground as a writer when I could find little.

—Michelle Latiolais
7 *September 2010*
Ucross, Wyoming

"Caduceus" *The Northwest Review*, Winter 2009 (Nominated for a Pushcart Prize)

"Crazy" *The Iowa Review*, December 2008

"Damned Spot" *Woof! Writers on Dogs*, Viking 2008

"Place" *Green Mountains Review* spring 2008, Vol.XXI, No.1 (Nominated for a Pushcart Prize)

"Widow" *Western Humanities Review*, January 2007

"Boys" *Women On The Edge: Writing from Los Angeles*, fall 2005

"Breathe" *Zyzzyva*, spring 2002

"Thorns" *Santa Monica Review*, fall 2000

"Involutions" *The Antioch Review*, spring 2000

"Pink" *Santa Monica Review*, fall 1999

"The Moon," "The Long Table" and "Tattoo," *Santa Monica Review*, spring 1999

"The Legal Case" *Absolute Disaster*, Dove Press 1996